Dalton wrapped his arms around her waist and pulled her close. "You deserve a proper thank-you for taking care of me," he whispered as his mouth found hers.

His lips were warm and held a hint of whiskey. They were perfect. Her heart beat at record time. Her hands slid up to hold the ridge of his shoulders as Dalton pulled her tighter and the pressure of his mouth increased. Her body heated as if she were basking in the sun.

His tongue traced her lips. Her fingers seized his coat and she moaned. More...she wanted more. She returned his kiss.

Melanie had no idea how much time had passed by the time Dalton released her. Dazed, it took her a few seconds before she realized that someone was clapping.

"I think we're making a scene," Dalton said as he picked up his bag and took her arm, leading her toward the door.

She glanced around to see a family grinning at them. "I guess we are..."

The words came out sounding shaky. The warmth of his lips still lingered on hers. She still tingled all over. Not thinking about what she was doing, she ran her tongue along her bottom lip. His taste still lingered.

Dalton groaned. "Please don't do that."

"What?"

He leaned in close. "Lick your lips. If you do it again I might *really* make a public scene."

Dear Reader,

During the fall months of the year the focus in my house turns to American football. We spend hours watching and discussing it. We even attend games. While the males in my family are concerned with only what is happening on the field, I often think about what goes on behind the scenes. Who takes care of the players? What happens when a player gets hurt? During one of those games I wondered what it would be like if the team doctor was a woman, and how it would be for her to work in that man's world…

This is just what my character Melanie does in this story. For her, the game of football is a family affair. And when she has to call in an orthopaedic surgeon who cares nothing about the game for a second opinion, the fireworks explode.

I hope you enjoy reading my book as much as I enjoyed writing it. I love to hear from my readers. You can contact me at SusanCarlisle.com.

Susan

ONE NIGHT
BEFORE
CHRISTMAS

BY
SUSAN CARLISLE

MORAY COUNCIL LIBRARIES & INFO.SERVICES

20 39 91 84

Askews & Holts

RF RF

First published in Great Britain 2015
by Mills & Boon, an imprint of Harlequin (UK) Limited,
Eton House, 18-24 Paradise Road, Richmond, Surrey, TW9 1SR

© 2015 Susan Carlisle

ISBN: 978-0-263-25923-0

Susan Carlisle's love affair with books began when she made a bad grade in maths in the sixth grade. Not allowed to watch TV until she'd brought the grade up, she filled her time with books and became a voracious romance reader. She still has 'keepers' on the shelf to prove it. Because she loved the genre so much she decided to try her hand at creating her own romantic worlds. She still loves a good happily-ever-after-story. When not writing, Susan doubles as a high school substitute teacher, which she has been doing for sixteen years. Susan lives in Georgia with her husband of twenty-eight years and has four grown children. She loves castles, travelling, cross-stitching, hats, James Bond and hearing from her readers.

Books by Susan Carlisle

Mills & Boon Medical Romance

Heart of Mississippi
The Maverick Who Ruled Her Heart
The Doctor Who Made Her Love Again

Snowbound with Dr Delectable
NYC Angels: The Wallflower's Secret
Hot-Shot Doc Comes to Town
The Nurse He Shouldn't Notice
Heart Surgeon, Hero...Husband?
The Doctor's Redemption
His Best Friend's Baby

Visit the Author Profile page at
millsandboon.co.uk for more titles.

To Lacey.
Thanks for loving my son.

CHAPTER ONE

DR. MELANIE HYDE stood with the other chauffeurs waiting and watching passengers outside the security zone at the top of the escalators. Overhead the notes of "Jingle Bells" were being piped via speakers throughout Niagara Falls International Airport in upstate New York. She wiggled the small white sign she held back and forth. Written on it was *Reynolds*.

She was there to pick up the "go-to" orthopedic sports doctor. He'd been flown in on a private jet paid for by the Niagara Falls Currents, the professional football team and her employer. Her father, the general manager, had sent her on this mission in the hope that she might, in his words, "soften the doctor up."

Melanie had no idea how she was supposed to do that. She would have to find some way because she didn't want to disappoint her father. Long ago she'd accepted what was expected of her. Not that she always liked it.

Maybe the one physician to another respect would make Dr. Reynolds see the team's need to get Martin "The Rocket" Overtree on the field for the Sunday playoff game and hopefully the weeks after that.

As club physician, Melanie had given her professional opinion but her dad wanted a second one. That hurt, but she was a team player. Had been all her life. Just once she'd like her father to see her for who she really was: a smart woman who did her job well. An individual.

In the sports world, that orthopedic second opinion came in the form of Dr. Dalton Reynolds of the Reynolds Sports and Orthopedic Center, Miami, Florida.

She'd never seen him in person but she had read plenty of his papers on the care of knee and leg injuries. "The Rocket" had a knee issue but he wanted to play and Melanie was feeling the pressure from the head office to let him. More like her father's not so gentle nudge.

Having grown up in a football-loving world, she knew the win and, in major-league ball, the money, was everything. The burden to have "The Rocket" on the field was heavy. On the cusp of a chance to go to the Super Bowl, the team's star player was needed.

She shifted her heavy coat to the other arm and scanned the crowd of passengers streaming off the escalators for a male in his midfifties and wiggled the sign again.

A tall man with close-trimmed brown hair sporting a reddish tint, carrying a tan trench coat and a black bag, blocked her view. He was do-a-double-take handsome but Melanie shifted her weight to one foot and looked around him, continuing to search the crowd.

"I'm Reynolds," the man said in a deep, husky voice that vibrated through her. The man could whisper sweet nothings in her ear all day long.

Jerking back to a full standing position, she locked gazes with his unwavering one.

"Dr. Dalton Reynolds?"

"Yes."

His eyes were the color of rich melted chocolate but they held none of the warmth. He wasn't at all who she'd anticipated. Old and stuffy, instead of tall and handsome, was what she'd had in mind. This man couldn't be more than a few years older than her. He must be truly brilliant if he was the most eminent orthopedic surgeon in the country at his age.

"Uh, I wasn't expecting you to be so...young," she blurted.

He gave her a sober look. "I'm sorry to disappoint."

She blinked and cleared her throat. "I'm not disappointed, just surprised."

"Good, then. Shouldn't we be getting my luggage? I'd like to see the patient this evening."

With it being only a week before Christmas, he must be in a hurry to return home to his family. After a moment's hesitation she said, "I don't know if that'll be possible. The players may have gone home by the time we get back."

"I didn't come all this way to spend time in my hotel room. I have a practice in Miami to be concerned with." That statement was punctuated with a curl of one corner of his mouth.

He had a nice one. Why was she thinking about his mouth when she should be talking to him about Rocket? The off-center feeling she had around this stranger unnerved her. She worked in primarily a man's world all the time and never had this type of reaction to one of them.

They started walking toward the baggage area. As they did, Melanie put the sign she was still carrying in a garbage can, then pulled her phone out of her pocket. "I'll try and get Coach. Have him ask Rocket to hang around. But football players sometimes have minds of their own."

"I can appreciate that, Ms...?"

Melanie stopped and looked at him. He faced her, his broad shoulders blocking her view of the other people passing them.

She raised her chin. "I'm Dr. Melanie Hyde."

A flash of wonder flickered in his eyes.

Good. She'd managed to surprise him.

"Dr. Hyde, if Mr. Overtree expects my help he'll need

to be examined as soon as possible. I have patients at home who are trying to stay out of wheelchairs."

With that he turned and walked toward the revolving luggage rack.

Melanie gaped at him. So much for "smoothing him over."

Dalton had little patience for silly games. Even when they were played with attractive women. He'd been astonished to find out that the team doctor was female and the person who had been sent to pick him up. Usually that job fell to a hired driver or one of the team underlings. He had to admit she was the prettiest chauffeur he'd ever had.

As far as he was concerned, he was here to do a job and nothing more. He wasn't impressed by the game of football. The only aspect that drew him in was that he cared about helping people who were hurting. He'd been called in to examine an injured player at great expense. The money he earned, good money, from making these types of "house calls" was what he used to support his foundation. It oversaw struggling foster children with physical and mental issues, giving them extra care so they had a chance to succeed in life. He would continue to do this job as long as the teams paid him top dollar. However, he didn't buy into all the football hype.

He knew from experience that not everyone was cut out for games. He'd left that far behind, being constantly teased for being the "brain with no game." It had taken time and work on his part but he'd overcome his childhood. Now he was successful in his field, had friends and a good life. He had proven anyone could overcome their past. That was why he'd started the foundation. To give other kids a step in the right direction so they didn't struggle as he had.

The tall, athletic-looking doctor came to stand beside him. She almost met him eye to eye. He liked women with long legs. Glancing down while watching the baggage con-veyer as it circled in front of him, he confirmed the length of her legs. She wore a brown suit with a cream-colored blouse. There was nothing bold about her dress to make her stand out. Still, something about her pricked his in-terest. Her features were fine and her skin like porcelain, a complete contrast to her all-business appearance. Not of his usual fare—bleached blonde and heavy breasted— she looked more of the wholesome-girl-next-door variety. Under all that sweetness was there any fire?

He looked at the bags orbiting before him. *Football was still such a man's world, so why would a woman choose to become a football team doctor?*

His black leather duffel circled to him. He leaned over and picked it up. Slinging it over his shoulder, he turned to her. "I'm ready."

"This way, then." She pulled on the large down-stuffed coat she'd held. As she walked, she wrapped a knit scarf effortlessly around her neck and pulled a cap over her hair. He followed her. There was a nice sway to her hips. Even in the shapeless outfit she had a natural sex appeal. He shouldn't be having these sorts of thoughts because he wouldn't be here long enough to act on them.

The automatic glass doors opened, allowing in a blast of freezing-cold air that took his breath and made his teeth rattle. "Hold up." He stepped back inside.

She followed. He didn't miss the slight twitch at the corner of her full lips. She was laughing at him. He didn't like being laughed at.

He plopped his bag on the floor and set his shoulder bag beside it before putting on his trench coat.

"Is that the heaviest overcoat you have?" she asked.

Tying the belt at the waist, he looked directly at her. "Yes. There isn't much call for substantial clothes in Miami."

"I guess there isn't. Would you like to stop and get a warmer one on our way to the practice field?"

He shook his head as he picked up his bags again. "I don't plan to be here that long."

Again they headed out the door, Dalton tried to act as if the wind wasn't cutting right through his less-than-adequate clothes. Even with a shirt, sweater and coat he was miserable.

"Why don't you wait here and I'll circle around to get you?"

"No, I'm fine. Let's get moving." He bowed his head against the spit of icy rain.

Dalton had spent a lifetime of not appearing weak and he wouldn't change now. As the smart foster kid, he hadn't fit in at school or in the houses he'd been placed in. With a father in jail and a drug addict for a mother, he'd been in and out of homes for years. It wasn't until his mother died of an overdose that he'd stayed in one place for any length of time. At the Richies', life had been only marginally better before he was sent to another home.

He'd had plenty of food and clothes, but little about his life had been easy. When all the other kids were out playing, he was busy reading, escaping. The most miserable times were when he did join in a game. He was the last one chosen for the team. If finally picked, he then had to deal with the ridicule of being the worst player. He learned quickly not to show any weakness. As a medical student and now a surgeon, the honed trait served him well.

Football, freezing weather and a laughing woman, no matter how attractive she was, were not to his taste. He needed to do this consultation and get back to Florida.

Melanie couldn't help but find humor in the situation. Dr. Reynolds' long legs carried him at such a brisk pace, she had trouble staying in the lead enough to show him where the car was parked. He must be freezing. Niagara

Falls was not only known for the falls but for the horrible winter weather. What planet did he live on that he hadn't come prepared?

She pushed the button on her key fob, unlocking the car door as they approached so that he wouldn't have to wait any longer than necessary outside. Minutes later she had the car started and the heat blasting on high. She glanced at her passenger. He took a great deal of space in her small car. Almost to the point of overwhelming her. Why was he affecting her so? Melanie glanced at him. Judging by the tenseness of his square jaw, he must be gritting his teeth to keep them from chattering.

"I'm sure it'll be warm in a few minutes."

An *mmm* sound of acknowledgement came from his direction as Melanie pulled out into the evening traffic on the freeway.

Her phone rang. "Please excuse me. This may be the office about Rocket." She pushed the hands-free button. "This is Mel."

"Rocket is on his way back." Her father's booming voice filled the car.

"Great. I'm sure Dr. Reynolds will be glad to hear that. We should be there in about thirty minutes." Her father hung up and she asked her passenger, "Have you ever been to Niagara Falls?"

"No."

"Well, the falls are a beautiful sight any time of the year, but especially now with the snow surrounding them."

"I don't think I'll be here long enough to do much sight-seeing."

"It doesn't take much to say you've seen the falls. They're pretty large."

"What I came for is to see Mr. Overtree, so I imagine I should focus on that." Obviously he wasn't much for small talk or the local sights. Melanie stopped making an effort at conversation and concentrated on driving in the thickening snow and slow traffic. With her heavier clothes on, she began to get too warm but didn't want to turn down the heat for fear Dr. Reynolds needed it.

They were not far from the team camp when he said, "I don't think I've ever met a female team doctor before."

She'd long ago become used to hearing that statement. With a proud note in her voice she said, "As far as I know, I'm the only one in the NFL."

"What made you want to be a sports doctor?"

His voice, she bet, had mesmerized more than one woman. Where had that idea come from? What was his question? "I wanted to be a part of the world of football."

What it did was make her feel included. She'd grown up without a mother, a coach for a father and three brothers who now played professional football. In her family if you didn't eat, drink and live football you were left out. As a girl she couldn't play, so by becoming the team doctor she took her place as part of the team. Even when it wasn't her heart's desire. "Team means everything, Mel," her father would say. "That's what we are—a team." He would then hug her. To get his attention she learned early on what she needed to do as part of the team. As she grew older the pressure to be a team member grew and became harder to live with.

She often wondered what her father would say if she confessed she didn't want to belong to a team any longer. Sometimes she'd like to just be his daughter. She was afraid of what the repercussions might be. Still she would have to say she was happy, wouldn't she?

Melanie pulled the car into her designated parking space in front of the two-story, glass-windowed building. "Leave your bag in the car. I'll take you to the hotel after we're through here."

Dr. Reynolds nodded and climbed out. He wasn't large like some of the players but he did look like a man who could hold his own in a fight. With those wide shoulders and trim hips, he appeared physically fit.

"This way," she said as they entered the lobby. The space was built to impress. With hardwood floors, bright lights and the Currents' mascot and bolt of lightning painted on the wall, the place did not disappoint. No matter how many times Melanie entered this direction, she had a moment of awe. She enjoyed her job, liked the men she worked with and loved the passion of the crowd when the Currents took the field to play.

Dr. Reynolds followed her through security and down the hall to the elevator. There they waited in silence until the doors opened and they entered. She pushed the button that would take them to the bottom floor where the Athlete Performance Area and her office were located. When the elevator opened she led him along a hall painted with different football players making moves. "Rocket should be back here."

The team had a state-of-the-art workout facility, from whirlpool and sauna to a walking pool and all the other equipment on the market to help improve the human body. She was proud of the care she was able to provide for the men. Two years ago she had instituted a wellness program for retired players who continued to live nearby.

She pushed open the double swinging doors and entered her domain. Here she normally had the final say.

Rocket was already there, sitting on the exam table. Wearing practice shorts and a T-shirt with the sleeves cut out of it, he looked like the football player he was. What didn't show was the injury to his knee and his importance to the Currents winning a trip to the Super Bowl.

She pulled off her coat. "Rocket, sorry to pull you back in but Dr. Reynolds wanted to see you right away." Turning to Dr. Reynolds, she said, "This is Rocket—or Martin Overtree. Rocket, Dr. Reynolds."

The two men shook hands.

"Thanks for coming, Doc," Rocket said. "Mel says you're the man to help keep me on the field."

"I don't know about that. I'll need to examine you first." Dr. Reynolds pulled off his coat.

"I'll take that," Melanie offered and draped it over a chair in the corner.

The doctor rolled up his shirtsleeves, revealing tanned arms with a dusting of dark hair. Using his foot, he pulled a rolling stool from where it rested near the exam table. He straddled it and rolled to the end of the table. "I'm going to do some movements and I want you to tell me when or if they hurt and where."

Melanie watched as the doctor placed his large hands on either side of the huge running back's dark-skinned knee. With more patience than he'd shown at the airport, he examined it. Rocket grunted occasionally when Dr. Reynolds moved his knee a certain way.

The doctor pushed with his heels, putting space between him and the patient. "Now, Mr. Overtree—"

"Make it Rocket. Everyone else does."

Dr. Reynolds seemed to hesitate a second before he said in a stilted tone, "Rocket, I'd like you to lift your foot as far as you can without your knee hurting."

Rocket followed his instructions. The grimace on the player's face when his leg was almost completely extended said the knee might be in worse shape than Melanie had feared.

Dr. Reynolds placed his hand on the top of the knee.

She'd always had a thing for men's hands. To her they were a sign of their character. Dr. Reynolds had hands with long tapered fingers and closely cut nails that said he knew what he was doing and he could be trusted. Melanie liked what they said about him.

He moved his fingers over Rocket's knee. "That's good. Have you had a hard hit to this knee recently?"

Rocket made a dry chuckle. "Doc, I play football. I'm getting hit all the time."

"Yeah, I know who you are. But has there been one in particular you can remember?"

"A couple weeks ago in the game I was coming down, and the safety and I got tangled up pretty good."

Melanie had learned early in her career as a team doctor that many of the players, no matter how large, were deep down gentle giants. Often they had a hard time showing weakness and fear. Rocket was one of those guys. Melanie was grateful to the doctor for his compassionate care.

"Any popping sensation, swelling or pain?"

"Not really. If Doc here—" Rocket indicated Melanie "—hadn't pulled me off the machine the other day I wouldn't have really noticed. Players are in some kind of pain all the time if they play ball. We get to where we don't really notice."

Dr. Reynolds gave him a thoughtful nod and stood. "I'd like to get some X-rays and possibly a MRI before I confirm my diagnosis."

"I'll set them up." Melanie made a note on the pad at her desk.

The double doors burst wide open. Her father entered. In his booming voice he demanded, "Well, Doc, is Rocket going to be able to play on Sunday?"

Melanie flinched. Based on what she knew about Dr. Reynolds in their short acquaintance, he wouldn't take kindly to being pressured.

Reynolds looked her father straight in the eyes. "It's Dr. Dalton Reynolds." Not the least bit intimidated, he continued, "And you are?"

Her father pulled up short. Silence ping-ponged around the room. Few people, if any, dared to speak to her father in that manner. When he was a coach he had insisted on respect and as general manager he commanded it.

"Leon Hyde, general manager of the Currents." He offered his hand.

Dr. Reynolds gave her a questioning look, then accepted her father's hand. The moment of awkwardness between the two men disappeared as the doctor met her usually intimidating father toe to toe.

She couldn't remember another man who hadn't at least been initially unsettled by her father. Dr. Reynolds's gaze didn't waver. Her appraisal of him rose.

"So, Dr. Reynolds, is Rocket going to be able to run for us Sunday?" her father asked with a note of expectancy in his voice.

"I need to look at the X-rays and MRI before I can let you know."

"That'll be in the morning," Melanie said.

"Good." Her father turned to her. "Mel, we need Rocket on the field."

"I understand." She did, but she wasn't sure her father wasn't more concerned about winning than he was Rocket's health. She just hoped it didn't come down to her having to choose between the team and her professional conscience. "But I must consider Rocket's well-being. I won't sign off until Dr. Reynolds has made his determination."

Her father gave her a pointed look. The one she recognized that came before the team player speech.

Instead he continued, "You'll see that Dr. Reynolds gets to the Lodge and is comfortable, won't you?"

As always, it wasn't a question but a directive. She nodded. "Yes."

"Good." He looked at Dr. Reynolds. "I anticipate a positive report in the morning."

The doctor made no commitment.

Her father then gave Rocket a slight slap on the shoulder. "Go home and take care of that knee. We need you on the field Sunday."

Melanie watched the doors swing closed as her father exited. She was impressed by Dr. Reynolds's ability not to appear pushed into making a decision. Her father was known for being a persuasive man and getting what he wanted. He wanted Rocket to play Sunday. Dr. Reynolds didn't act as if he would be a yes-man if he didn't feel it was safe for Rocket to do so. On this she could agree with him.

Still, it hurt that her father didn't trust her opinion.

Dalton pulled the collar of his coat farther up around his neck and hunched his shoulders. They were in her car, moving through what was now a steady snowfall. It was unbearably cold. Even the car heater didn't seem to block the chill seeping into his bones.

Dr. Hyde leaned forward and adjusted the thermostat on the dashboard. "It should be warm in here soon."

He wasn't sure he'd ever be comfortable again. Thankfully, a few minutes later he began to thaw. She maneuvered along the road with the confidence of a person who had done this many times.

"We should be at the Lodge in about half an hour. Would you like to stop for something to eat? The Lodge does have an excellent restaurant if you'd rather wait."

He looked out the windshield. "I don't think I'm interested in being out in this weather any longer than necessary."

"It does require getting used to."

He couldn't imagine that happening either. "Why is Mr. Overtree called The Rocket?"

She glanced at him and chuckled lightly. "You apparently have never seen him play. He's fast. Very fast."

"I've never seen a professional football game."

Melanie looked at him. The car swerved for a second before she corrected it.

"You might want to watch the road."

She focused on the road again. "You've never seen one in person? Or on TV?"

"Neither. No interest. I have a busy practice."

"You have to be kidding! Football is America's game." She sounded as if she was going to get overly excited about the subject.

"I think it's baseball that's supposed to be the 'all-American game.'"

"It might have been at one time but no longer." The words were said as if she dared anyone to contradict her.

He couldn't help but raise a brow. "I think there are a lot of people who love baseball that might disagree with you."

"Maybe but I bet most of them watch the Super Bowl."

Dr. Reynolds gave a loud humph. "I understand that most watch for the halftime show and the commercials." He didn't miss the death grip she had on the stirring wheel. She really took football seriously. It was time to move on to a new subject or ask to drive. "The general manager's name is Hyde. Any relation?"

"My father."

"Isn't that a conflict of interest?"

She glanced at him again. "Normally, no. We're so close to going to the playoffs that everyone on the team, including my father, is wound up tight. Anyway, most of my work is directly with the coach."

Based on the way her father spoke to her, she'd agree with him if Dalton declared Rocket shouldn't play. His being asked to consult seemed necessary just to make the team look as if they were truly interested in the player's health. So far, all he could tell they were concerned about was winning the next game.

"What made you decide to be a team doctor?"

"With brothers playing in the NFL and a father who coached, it's the family business. I always wanted to be a doctor and being a team doctor gave me a chance to be a part of football," she said in a flat tone.

Was there more going on behind that statement?

The concept of family, much less a family business, was foreign to him. His family's occupation had been selling drugs and he'd wanted to get as far away from it as he could. He'd been a loner and alone for as long as he could remember.

Thankfully she turned into a curving road lined with large trees and had to concentrate on her driving. A few minutes later, they approached a three-story split-cedar building. She pulled under a portico with small lights hanging from it. Two large trees dressed in the same lights with red bows flanked the double wood-framed doors.

"This is Poospatuck Lodge. I think you'll be comfortable here. The team keeps a suite."

"Poospatuck?" When had he become such an inquisitive person? Usually on these trips he did what was required without any interest in the area he was visiting.

"It's an Indian tribe native to New York."

As she opened the door Dalton said, "It's not necessary for you to get out."

"I don't mind. I need to speak to the management and I can show you up to your suite."

Dalton grabbed his two bags from the backseat and followed her through the door into the welcome heat of the lobby. Large beams supported the two-story ceiling. Glass filled the wall above the door. The twinkle of lights from outside filtered in through the high windows. Flames burned bright in a gray rock fireplace taking up half of one wall. Above it was a large wreath. Along the mantel lay greenery interspersed with red candles. A grand stairway with an iron handrail led to the second floor.

Christmas had never been a big holiday for him. As a small child, it had just been another day for his parents to shoot up and pass out. In fact, the last time he was taken from his mother had been the day before Christmas. It hadn't been much fun spending Christmas Day at a stranger's house. Being a foster child on that day just sent the signal more strongly that he wasn't a real member of the family. Some of his foster parents had really tried to make him feel a part of the unit but it had never really worked. Now it was just another day and he spent it on the beach or with friends.

Dr. Hyde walked toward the registration desk located to the right of the front door.

The clerk wore a friendly smile. "Hello, Dr. Hyde. Nice to see you again."

"Hi, Mark. It's good to see you also. How's your family doing?"

"Very well, thank you."

"Good." She glanced back. "This is Dr. Reynolds. He'll be staying in our suite. I'll show him up."

"Very good. It's all ready for you."

She turned to Dalton. "The elevator is over this way but we're only going to the second floor if you don't mind carrying your bags."

"I believe I can manage to go up the stairs."

She gave him an apologetic look. "I didn't mean to imply..."

"Please just show me my room." Dalton picked up his bags off the floor where he'd placed them earlier. He didn't miss her small sound of disgust as she turned and walked toward the stairs. He followed three or four steps behind as they climbed the stairs. He enjoyed the nice sway of her hips.

At the top of the stairs she turned left and continued down a wide, well lit hallway to the end.

A brass plaque on the door read Niagara Currents. She pulled a plastic door key out of her handbag. With a quick swipe through the slot, she opened the door. Entering, she held the door for him.

He stepped into the seating area. The space had a rustic feel to it that matched the rest of the building. The two sofas and couple of chairs looked comfortable and inviting.

"Your bedroom is through here." She pushed two French windows wide to reveal a large bed. "This is my favorite part of the suite."

He didn't say anything. She turned and looked at him. Dalton raised a brow. A blush crept up her neck.

"Um, I like the view from here is what I meant to say. The falls are incredible."

Dalton moved to stand in the doorway. A large window filled the entire wall. He could just make out the snow falling from the light coming from below.

"There's an amazing view of the falls from here. Now you can say you saw the falls."

"So do you stay here often?"

She glared at him. "What're you implying, Dr. Reynolds?"

"I was implying nothing, Dr. Hyde. I just thought you must have stayed overnight if you were that well acquainted with the view."

"This suite is sometimes used for meetings. Now, if you'll excuse me, I need to be getting home. I'll be here at eight-thirty in the morning to pick you up."

"Why not earlier?"

"Because the X-rays won't be ready until nine. So just enjoy your evening. If you need anything, ask for Mark."

"I shouldn't call you?" he said in a suggestive tone, just to see how she would react. Dr. Hyde pursed her lips. Was she on the verge of saying something?

After a moment, she looked through her handbag and pulled out a card. She handed it to him. "If you need me, you may. Good night."

The door closed with a soft click behind her.

Why had he needled her? It was so unlike him. Maybe it was because she'd questioned his clothing decisions.

She'd been polite about it but there was still an undercurrent of humor. Could he possibly want her to feel a little out of sorts too? He had to admit it had been interesting to make her uncomfortable.

CHAPTER TWO

MELANIE PULLED IN front of the Lodge at eight-thirty the next morning. The snow had stopped during the night but the sky was overcast as if it would start again soon. She'd left last night uncomfortable about Dr. Reynolds' suggestive manner. She wasn't feeling any better about being his hostess this morning.

When his dark shapely brow had risen as if she were proposing she might be staying the night with him, she'd been insulted for a second. Then a tinge of self-satisfaction had shot through her that a male had noticed her. She'd had her share of boyfriends when she'd been young but recently the men attracted to her had become fewer. They seemed frightened by her position or were only interested so they could meet either one of her famous brothers or one of the Currents players. The one that she had loved hadn't truly cared for her. She'd known rejection and wanted no part of it.

There had been one special man. He was a lawyer for a player. She couldn't have asked for someone who fit into her family better. He lived and breathed football. They had even talked of marriage. It wasn't until he started hinting, then asking her to put a good word in with her father when an assistant manager's job came open that she realized he was using her. When she refused to do so, he dumped her. It had taken her months after that to even accept a friendly date. After that experience she judged every man that showed any attention to her with a sharp eye. She wouldn't go through something like that again. Dr. Reynolds might flirt with her but she would see to it that was all that would happen. A fly in, fly out guy was someone she had no interest in.

She entered the lobby to find Dr. Reynolds waiting in one of the many large armchairs near the fireplace. Was he fortifying himself for the weather outside? She smiled. He had looked rather pitiful the night before in his effort to stay warm.

This morning his outfit wasn't much better. Wearing a dress shirt, jeans and loafers, he didn't look any more prepared for the weather than he had yesterday. In reality, it was unrealistic to expect him to buy clothes just to fly to Niagara Falls to see Rocket but he would be cold. However, he was undoubtedly the most handsome man she'd ever met. His striking good looks drew the attention of a couple of women who walked by. He had an air of self-confidence about him.

His head turned and his midnight gaze found her. His eyes were his most striking attribute. The dark color was appealing but it was the intensity of his focus that held her. As if he saw beyond what was on the surface and in some way understood what was beneath.

His bags sat on the floor beside him. She didn't have to ask if he had plans to return to the sun and fun as soon as possible. If Rocket needed surgery he would have to go to Miami to have it done. She hoped that wouldn't be the case but feared otherwise.

"Dr. Reynolds, good morning," she said as she approached.

He stood, picked up his shoulder bag and slipped it over his neck. Grabbing his other bag, he walked toward her.

Apparently he was eager to leave. She stepped closer. "Have you had breakfast?"

"I ate a couple of hours ago."

So he was an early riser. "Then we can go." Melanie turned and headed back the way she had come. By the time she settled behind the steering wheel, he'd placed his bag in the backseat and was buckling up.

As she pulled out onto the main road, he said, "Well, at least it isn't snowing."

"No, but the weatherman is calling for more. A lot more."

"Then I need to see Mr. Overtree's X-rays and get to the airport."

"Only eight more days. You must be in a hurry to get home to your family for Christmas."

"No family. I'll be working."

"Oh." Despite her family's year-round focus on football, they all managed to come together during the holidays. Sometimes it was around Christmas Day games, but they always found a time that worked for all of them. Her brothers had wives and children, and the crowd was rowdy and loud. She loved it. Melanie couldn't imagine not having any family or someone to share the day with. Even though much of the work fell to her. The men in her life expected her to organize and take care of them. She'd never let them know that sometimes she resented them taking her for granted.

They rode in silence for a while. He broke it by asking, "How much longer?"

"It should be only another ten minutes or so."

The sky had turned gray and a large snowflake hit the windshield. By the time she pulled into the team compound it had become a steady snow shower. Instead of parking in the front, this time she pulled through the gate to the back of the building and parked in the slot with her name painted on it. Thankfully, her spot was close to the door so they wouldn't have far to walk.

Dr. Reynolds huddled in his coat on their way to the

door. With his head down, he walked slowly as if in an effort not to slip on the ice and snow. Melanie stayed close behind him. She had no idea what her plan was if he started to go down. Inside, they both took off their jackets and shook them out.

"I'll take that," Melanie said. Dr. Reynolds handed her his overcoat. Their hands brushed as she reached for it. A tingle of awareness went up her spine. Shaking it off, she hung their coats up on pegs along the wall and headed down the hall. "This way."

"I assume Mr. Overtree's X-rays will have been sent to your computer in the exam room. The MRI as well."

"Yes."

She made a turn and went down another hallway until she reached the Athlete Performance Area and pushed open one of the swinging doors and held it. She let him have the door, then continued into the room. Rocket, Coach Rizzo and her father were already there.

Her father gave her a questioning look. She shrugged her shoulder. Surely her father wouldn't push Dr. Reynolds to agree to let Rocket play if the test indicated that he shouldn't. As team doctor, she had the final say anyway. She would refuse to be a team player if it came down to Rocket's long-term health. Moving on to her desk, she flipped on the computer. She pulled up Rocket's chart. "Dr. Reynolds, the X-rays from last week and his most recent ones are ready for your review."

Giving her what she could only describe as an impressed look, Dr. Reynolds seemed to appreciate her being efficient and prepared. For some reason that made her feel good. The kind of respect she didn't feel she received from her father. She stepped away from the desk to allow him room. When the other men moved to join them, she shook her head, indicating they should give Dr. Reynolds some space. Despite that, her father still took steps toward her desk.

"Thank you, Doctor. You've been very thorough," Dr. Reynolds said to her.

It was nice to be valued as a fellow medical professional who was more interested in the health of the player than whether or not the team won. She and Dr. Reynolds were at least in the same playbook where that was concerned.

In her mind no game was worth a man losing mobility for the rest of his life. A player's heath came first in that regard. She was sure her father and the coach didn't feel the same. More than once she'd been afraid that there might be repercussions from them if she placed a player on the disabled list. Even the players gave her a hard time about her being overly cautious. As their doctor, the players' health took precedence over winning a game. Rocket had his sights set on being the most valuable player. He might agree to anything to get it. Even playing when he was injured. Sometimes she felt as if she had the most rational mind in the group.

Dr. Reynolds took her chair. He gave that same concentrated consideration to the screen as he seemed to give everything. With a movement of one long finger, he clicked through the black-and-white screens of different X-ray angles of Rocket's knee. He studied them all but made no comment.

He turned to her. "Did you have a MRI done?"

She nodded.

"Good. I'd like to see it."

She moved to the desk and he pushed back enough to allow her to get to the keyboard. As she punched keys she was far too aware of him close behind her. Her fingers fumbled on the keys but seconds later she had the red-and-blue images on the screen.

Minutes went by as Dr. Reynolds moved through the different shots.

"Well?" her father snapped.

"Let him have time to look," Melanie said in an effort to placate him. Her father shot her a sharp look.

Dr. Reynolds continued to spend time on the side views of the knee. The entire room seemed to hold their collective breath as he spun in the chair. His gaze went to Rocket. "It looks like you have a one-degree patellar-tendon tear."

That was what she had been afraid of. "That was my diagnosis."

Dr. Reynolds nodded in her direction.

"We still needed a second opinion," her father said as he stepped back.

For once it would be nice for her father to appreciate her knowledge and ability.

"Can he play?" Coach Rizzo asked.

"The question is—*should* he play?" Then, to Rocket, Dr. Reynolds said, "Do you want to take the chance on ruining your knee altogether? I wouldn't recommend it. Let it rest, heal. You'll be ready to go next year."

The other men let go simultaneous groans.

Rocket moaned. "This is our year. Who's to know what'll happen next year?"

Her father looked at Rocket. "What do you want to do? Think about the bonus and the ring."

How like her father to apply pressure.

Dr. Reynolds looked at him. "Mr. Hyde, this is a decision that Rocket needs to make without any force."

Her father didn't look happy but he also didn't say anything more.

Rocket seemed not to know what the right answer was or, if he did, he didn't want to say it.

"Hey, Doc, what're the chances of it getting worse?" Rocket asked.

"If you take a hard hit, that'll be it. Your tendon is like a rope with a few of the strands frayed and ragged. You take a solid shot and the rope may break. What I know is that it won't get any better if you play. One good twist during a run could possibly mean the end of your career."

Her father huffed. "Roger Morton with the Wildcats had surgery and returned better than ever."

"I'm not saying it isn't possible. However, not everyone does that well."

Coach Rizzo walked over to Rocket and put his hand on his shoulder, "I think 'The Rocket' has what it takes to play for us on Sunday."

Dr. Reynolds stood. "That'll be for Mr. Overtree to decide."

"You can't do anything more?" Rocket asked Dr. Reynolds.

He looked as if he wanted to say no but instead said, "I'd like to see you use the knee. See what kind of mobility you have."

Before Rocket had time to respond, Coach Rizzo spoke up. "Practice starts in about ten minutes."

"Mel, why don't you show Dr. Reynolds to the practice field?" her father suggested.

"Okay." Once again, she wasn't sure how being tour guide to the visiting doctor fell under her job description but she was a team player. She would do what she was asked. As she headed out the door she said over her shoulder, "Rocket, be sure and wear your knee brace."

She looked at Dr. Reynolds. "The practice field is out this way."

Dalton followed Melanie out a different set of double doors and into a hallway. At the elevator they went down to the ground floor. Once again she was wearing a very efficient-looking business suit. With her shapely, slender body it would seem she'd want to show it off; instead, she acted as if she sought to play down being a woman.

Her father sure was a domineering man. She seemed to do his bidding without question. He was afraid that if he hadn't been brought in for that second opinion, her father would have overridden any decision she made about Rocket. For a grown woman she seemed to still be trying to make daddy happy.

"We aren't going outside, are we?" he asked.

She grinned. "No. We have an indoor practice field. A full stadium without the stands. You should be warm enough in there."

"Good."

Melanie led them down a hallway and through two extralarge doors into a covered walkway. Seconds later they entered a large building.

They walked down one of the sidelines until they were near the forty-yard line. A few of the players wandered out on the field and started stretching. They wore shoulder pads under practice jerseys and shorts.

"Hey, Doc," a couple of the players yelled as they moved to the center of the field.

She called back to them by name. Dalton wasn't used to this type of familiarity with his patients. As a surgeon he usually saw them only a couple of times and never again.

It was still cooler than he liked inside the building. Dalton crossed his arms over his chest, tucking his hands under his arms.

Dr. Hyde must have noticed because she said, "It's not near as cold in here as outside but we can't keep it too warm because the players would overheat." Not surprisingly Melanie didn't seem affected by the temperature.

Rocket loped on the field from the direction of the dressing room. Dalton studied the movement of his leg and so far couldn't see anything significantly out of the norm.

Melanie leaned toward him. "They'll go through their warm-up and then move into some skill work. I think that'll be when you can tell more about his knee. In the past he seemed to show no indication there might be a problem until he was running post plays."

"Post plays?"

"When they run up the field and then cut sharply one way or another."

He nodded and went back to learning Rocket's movements. *Rocket.* He shook his head. It seemed as if he was picking up the slang of the game.

Would Dr. Hyde agree with him if he said that Rocket didn't need to play? As a medical doctor, how could she not?

They had been standing there twenty minutes or so, him watching Rocket while Melanie spoke with every one of the big men who passed by. The staff along the sidelines with them did the same. She was obviously well liked.

The next time a guy came by her, Dalton asked, "You have a good relationship with the team. Does anyone not like you?"

A broad smile came to her face. "We're pretty much like family around here. We all have a job to do but most of us are really good friends. I work at having a positive relationship with the players. I try to have them see me as part of the team. I want them to feel comfortable coming to me with problems. Men tend to drag their feet about asking for help." He must have made a face because she said, "Not all, but I want them to come to me or one of the trainers before a problem gets so bad they can't play."

Dalton had nothing to base that type of camaraderie on. Long ago he'd given up on that idea. Unable to think of anything to say, he muttered, "That makes sense."

She touched his arm. Her small hand left a warm place behind when she removed it to point at Rocket. "Watch him when he makes this move."

The hesitation was so minor that Dalton might have missed it if he hadn't been looking as she instructed.

"Did you see it?"

"I did. It was almost as if he didn't realize he did it." He was impressed that she had caught it to begin with.

"Exactly. I noticed it during one practice. Called him in and did X-rays. Dad insisted I contact you. We can't afford for Rocket to be out."

He looked at her. "Afford?"

She continued to watch the action on the field. "Yeah. This is big business for the team as well as for all these guys' careers."

He looked at Rocket and made no effort to keep the skepticism out of his voice when he asked, "No life after football?"

She stepped back and gave him a sharp look. "Yes. That's the point. A successful season means endorsements, which means money in their pockets. That doesn't even include the franchise."

"And all this hinges on Rocket?"

"No, but he's an important part." She looked around and leaned so close he could smell her shampoo. "The star—for now."

He wasn't convinced but he nodded and said, "I think I get it."

Melanie's expression implied she wasn't sure he did.

They continued to watch practice from the edge of the sideline. The team was playing on the far end of the field.

"How long has Rocket...?" he began.

She turned to look at him.

Over her shoulder he saw a huge player barreling in their direction. His helmeted head was turned away as he looked at the ball in the air. Not thinking twice, Dalton wrapped his arms around Melanie and swiveled to the side so he would take the brunt of the hit. Slammed with a force he would later swear was the equivalent of a speeding train, his breath swooshed from his lungs. His arms remained around Melanie as they went through the air and landed on the Astroturf floor with a thud. The landing felt almost as hard as the original hit. He and Melanie ended up a tangle of legs and arms as the player stumbled over their bodies.

There was no movement from the soft form in his arms. Fear seized him. Had she been hurt? A moan brushed his cheek. At least she was alive. He loosened his hold and rolled to his side but his hands remained in place. Searching Melanie's face, he watched as her eyes fluttered open. She stared at him with a look of uncertainty.

"What…what happened?"

Dalton drew in a breath, causing his chest to complain. He would be in considerable pain in the morning. "We got hit."

"By what?"

"Doc Mel, you okay?" a player asked from above them.

Dalton looked up to find players and staff circling them.

A large man with bulging biceps sounded as if he might cry.

"I'm sorry, Doc Mel. Are you okay? I tried to stop." If that had been his idea of slowing down, Dalton would have hated being on the receiving end of the player's full power. Dalton returned his attention to Melanie. One of his hands rested beneath her shoulder and the other on her stomach. Her cheek was against his lips. "Do you think you can stand?"

"Why did you grab me?"

"Because you could have been hurt if I hadn't." Didn't she understand he might have just saved her life?

"Hurt?" She turned her head toward him. Her eyes were still dazed. "You have pretty eyes."

Dalton swallowed hard, which did nothing to ease the pain in his chest. She must have a head injury because he couldn't imagine her saying something so forward.

"Lie right where you are," one of the people above them commanded. "An ambulance is on its way."

Dalton shifted. "I don't think that's necessary."

The trainer said, "Yes, it is. You both need to be checked out."

"Look, I'm a doctor. I would know if I need…"

"Now you're a patient." A man with a staff shirt said, "Mel, where do you hurt?"

Dalton's hand moved to her waist and gave it a gentle shake. "Dr. Hyde, can you move?"

"Melanie…my name is Melanie," she murmured.

Three of the trainers shifted to one side of her and placed their arms under her, preparing to lift her enough to separate them.

"Melanie, they're going to move you." Dalton took his hands away.

She nodded then made a noise of acceptance and the trainers went to work. Dalton started to rise and a couple of the trainers placed their hands on his shoulders, stopping him.

A few minutes later the sound of the ambulances arriving caught his attention.

Melanie wasn't clear on all that had occurred before she woke up in the brightly lit emergency room.

"What's going on?" She looked at David, one of the trainers, who was sitting in a chair across the room.

"You were in an accident on the practice field."

Before David could elaborate, a white-haired doctor entered. "So, how are you feeling?" He stepped close to the bed and pulled out a penlight.

Slowly the events came back to her. She started to sit up. "How is Dr. Reynolds?"

The doctor pushed her shoulder, making her lie back. "First let me do my examination, then you can go check on him."

She settled back.

"I'll be in the waiting room," David said and went out the door.

"Now tell me what happened," the doctor said as he lifted one of her eyelids.

Melanie relayed the events she recalled and finished with "and Dr. Reynolds took the impact of the hit."

The doctor nodded thoughtfully. "That he did."

"How bad is he?"

"If you'll give me a few minutes to finish my exam you can go see for yourself."

Melanie's chest tightened. She hoped he wasn't badly hurt. Thankfully, the doctor pronounced her well enough to go. The time that she waited for the nurse with the discharge papers only made her anxiety grow. Because of her, Dalton was hurt.

"What exam room is Dr. Reynolds in?" Melanie asked as she pulled on her shoes.

"Next door." The nurse indicated to the right.

"Thanks." Melanie rose slowly, still feeling dazed. She sat on the edge of the bed for a few seconds. Her body would be sore tomorrow.

Minutes later, she knocked on the glass sliding door to the exam room. At a weak, "Come in," she entered. Dalton still wore his slacks but no shirt. He had a nicely muscled chest. She groaned when she saw the ice pack resting on his left rib cage. His eyes were glazed as if he were in pain and his lips were drawn into a tight line. Guilt filled her.

Another one of the trainers stood in the corner of the room, typing on his cell phone. When she entered he slipped out, giving her the impression he was relieved to do so.

"Hey," she said softly.

Dalton's response came out more as a grumble than a word.

Melanie stepped farther into the room. She had to let him know how much she appreciated what he'd done. "Thank you."

He nodded but his jaw remained tight.

"How are you?"

"I've been better." The words were uttered between clenched teeth.

A stab of remorse plunged through her. He was here because of her. She approached the bed and moved to put her hand on his shoulder, then stopped herself. That would be far too personal. "Don't talk if it hurts too much."

A nurse entered.

Melanie didn't give her time to pick up the chart before she asked, "How is he?" She had to find out something about his injuries without him having to do the speaking.

The nurse looked at him. "Do I have permission to discuss your case?"

He nodded.

"The doctor has some bruised ribs. He'll be sore for a week or so but nothing more serious."

At least that was positive news. Melanie was already guilt ridden enough. "Then he will be released?"

"He'll be released as soon as he has someone who can take him home and stay with him. He isn't going to feel like doing much for a few days."

"I'll see that he gets the care he needs," Melanie assured her.

Dalton's eyebrows went up. "Plane…"

The nurse placed the blood pressure cuff around his arm. "You don't need to be flying. I don't think you could stand the pain."

There was a knock at the door and Melanie looked away from Dalton to find John Horvitz, her father's right-hand man, standing there.

"How're you both doing?" Obviously he would be concerned about the visiting doctor being hurt on team time.

Melanie gave John a brief report. "He's in so much pain, it's difficult to speak." Dalton gave her a grateful look.

John focused his attention on her. "Your father wanted

me to check on you both. He had a meeting. I'll be giving him a full report."

And he would. That was always the way it had been. Her father sent someone else. When he'd coached, team issues took precedence. As the general manager, it wasn't any better. His concern had always come through a subordinate. What would it be like to have him show he really cared?

"He'll call when the meeting is over," John finished.

"Who hit us?" she asked.

John grimaced. "I was told it was Juice."

"He must have been flying!"

"Not 'Freight Train'?" Dalton mumbled.

Melanie laughed. The poor guy. Maybe he did have a sense of humor. She wrapped her arms around her waist when the laughter led to throbbing.

"Are you sure you're okay?" John asked her.

"Sore, but nothing that I can't stand. Dr. Reynolds is the one we should be worried about. I think we would both like to get out of here."

As if on cue, the ER doctor came in. "If you'll give me a few minutes, I'll see you have your discharge papers. There will be no driving or flying for two days."

Dalton partially sat up, "Two days!" As if the effort was too much for him, he fell back, closing his eyes.

She owed him for making sure she hadn't really got hurt but this was a busy time of the year and adding the Currents' play-off game didn't make it better. Now she was being saddled with taking care of him for two more days.

"The team will see that you are as comfortable as possible," John assured him.

Dalton's eyes opened but he said nothing.

John continued, "There's a driver and a car waiting to take you both home. I have notified the Lodge to do everything they can to make your stay comfortable."

"I'll see that he's well taken care of. Thanks, John," Melanie said.

Half an hour later, Melanie sucked in her breath when she looked out the hospital sliding glass door. Snow fell so thickly that she could just make out the cars in the parking lot. "The snow has really picked up."

Their driver waited under the pickup area with the engine running. Dr. Reynolds, always the gentleman, allowed her to get in the backseat first. Wincing as he bent to climb in, he joined her. He reached out to pull the door closed and groaned.

"Let me help." She leaned across him. Her chest brushed his as she stretched. His body heat mixed with the air blasting out of the car vents, making her too warm. He smelled like a fir after a misty rain. She stopped herself from inhaling. Using her fingertips, she managed to pull the door closed. His breath brushed her cheek as she sat up again, causing her midsection to flutter.

The windshield wipers swished back and forth in a rapid movement but the snow continued to pile up on the glass. She glanced at Dr. Reynolds. His shoulders were hunched and he was peering out with a concerned look on his face.

"Normal?" The word came out with a wince.

"We get a lot of snow here. We're used to it. Looks like we'll have a white Christmas, with it only being seven days off." She tried to make the last sentence sound upbeat. In pain, he took on an almost boyish look that had her heart going out to him.

He leaned back and closed his eyes. "Only thing white at Christmastime where I come from is the beach."

That didn't sound all that festive to her. Snow, a green tree, a warm fire and people you loved surrounding you was what she thought Christmas should be. She loved this time of the year.

The driver had the radio playing low and after the song

finished the announcer came on. "Fellow Niagarans, it's a white one out there. The good news is the roads are still passable and the airport open. But not sure it will be tomorrow. The storm isn't over yet."

Dalton moaned.

"I'm sorry for this inconvenience, Dr. Reynolds. Maybe in a few days you'll be up to going home," Melanie said in a sympathetic tone.

And she wouldn't be nursemaiding him anymore. She needed to talk to her father about what her duties as team doctor entailed. It would probably be a waste of time; he'd never listened to her in the past and wasn't likely to do so now.

Dalton questioned if the stars were aligned against him. He was stuck in Niagara Falls longer than he'd planned. Too long for his comfort. The driver pulled under the awning of the Lodge. Dalton opened the door despite the pain it brought and climbed out. It wasn't until he turned to close the door that he saw Dr. Hyde getting out.

"What're you doing?" he muttered through tightly clamped teeth.

"I'm going to stay and see about you tonight."

"What?"

"Didn't you hear the doctor? You need someone to check on you regularly over the next twenty-four hours."

"I'll be fine."

"For heaven's sakes, can we go inside to argue about this?"

Without another word, he turned and pulled open the door to the Lodge. He had to admit it required a great deal of effort to do so.

She came to stand beside him. "You obviously need help. I feel guilty enough about you getting hurt. The least I can do is make sure you're okay."

His look met hers for the first time since they'd left the

hospital. He wasn't used to seeing concern for him in any-one's eyes. He tried to take a deep breath. Pain shot through his side. He reluctantly said, "I would appreciate help."

"Then let's go try to make you as comfortable as you can be with those ribs. The elevator is over this way." They walked across the lobby.

"Not going to make me climb the stairs?" Each word pained him but he couldn't stop himself from making the comment.

She glared at him. "I thought your ribs hurt too much to speak."

He started to laugh and immediately wrapped his arms across his chest.

They rode the elevator up and walked to the room. At the door Melanie took out a room key.

"You have a key to my room?" Dalton asked with a hint of suspicion.

"I was given one when we knew you were coming so I could check on the room before you arrived." She slid the plastic card in the slot and opened the door. "I'm sure you're ready to lie down. I'll call for some food."

"Are you always so bossy?"

Melanie dropped her pocketbook into the closest chair. "I guess I am when it comes to taking care of my patients."

Dalton started toward the bedroom. "I'm not one of your patients."

"You are for the next twenty-four hours."

He wasn't pleased with the arrangements. Still, some-thing about having her concerned for him gave him an unfamiliar warm feeling. He'd never had anyone's total focus before. Mrs. Richie had been the only foster mother who came close to doing that, but he hadn't been there long before he heard her telling the social worker that it would be better for him to move to another house. After that he'd never let another woman know he hurt or see him in need. He made sure his relationships with women were short and remained at arm's length. All physical and no emotional involvement was the way he liked to keep things.

Dalton crossed the living space and circled one of the sofas that faced each other on his way to the bedroom on the left. There was another room on the opposite side of the large living area. He would leave that one for Melanie. Giving a brief glance to the minibar/kitchen area on the same side of the suite as the extra bedroom, he kept walking.

He ached all over. His jaw hurt from clamping his teeth in an effort not to show the amount of pain he was in. He'd learned as a child that if you let them see your weakness, they would use it against you. Now all he wanted to do was get a hot shower and go to bed.

Kicking off his shoes, he started to remove his knit pullover shirt and pain exploded through his side, taking his breath. For once in his life he had no choice but to ask for help. When his breath returned he opened the door and said, "Dr. Hyde?"

Melanie jumped up from the chair. She must have been watching for him. Hurrying toward him, her eyes were filled with concern, "Are you all right?"

"I need help with my shirt."

She stepped close. "Why do you need to take it off? You could lie down with it on."

"Shower."

"Oh."

"Help?"

"Sure. Sure." She didn't sound too confident as she followed him back into the room. When he stopped at the bed she reached for the hem of his shirt. Her blue eyes met his. There was a twinkle in her eyes when she said, "You know I'm usually on a first-name basis with people I help undress. You can feel free to call me Mel."

Was she flirting with him? "You said Melanie."

She gave him a questioning look.

"That's what you told me to call you after we were hit. You can call me Dalton."

"Dalton—" she said it as if she were testing the sound of it on her lips "—hold real still." She gathered the shirt until she had it under his arms.

Pain must have really addled his brain because he liked the sound of his name when she said it. He was just disappointed he didn't feel well enough to take advantage of her removing his clothes.

"Raise your hands as high as you can. I'll be as careful as I can but I'm afraid it's going to hurt."

He followed her directions. She wasn't wrong. It hurt like the devil as she worked the sleeves off. Sweat popped out on his forehead.

"I'm sorry. I'll get you something for the pain as soon as I'm done."

Dalton was exhausted by the time she finished.

"Let's go to the bathroom to remove your pants."

"I can do that."

"What's wrong? You afraid you have something I haven't seen? I'm a doctor for an all-male football team. I think I can handle removing your pants."

"You're not my doctor."

"Just as I expected. The double whammy. Who makes the worst patient? A male doctor."

He sneered, then walked gingerly into the bathroom and closed the door.

"Just the same, I'll be right out here if you need me," she called.

If nothing else she was tenacious. With more effort than he would have thought necessary, he managed to get his pants down. In the shower he stood under the hot water until he was afraid he might need Melanie's assistance to get out. That would be the ultimate humiliation—having to ask for help again. He already looked feeble as it was.

His clothes were not right for the weather, he was hurt

and now he needed her help to undress. He had to get a handle on the situation.

He turned the water off and stepped out of the shower. Melanie opened the door and entered just as he pulled a towel off the rack.

He stood motionless. "What're you doing here?"

She met his gaze with determination. "I'm going to help you dry off. There's no way you can handle that by yourself. If you're afraid I'll look, keep that bath sheet and I'll use one of the others."

Their standoff lasted seconds before he handed her his towel. He wouldn't be intimidated. Standing proudly in front of her, he didn't blink as she took the rectangular terry cloth. She circled behind him and ran the fabric across his shoulders then down his back.

His manhood twitched.

Melanie continued down his legs and up the front before she stepped around to face him. "Lean your head down."

Her voice sounded brisk and businesslike, as if she dried men off all the time. He rather liked having a woman dry him. Despite the pain he experienced with each breath, his body was reacting to the attention. Melanie briskly rubbed his hair, then went over his shoulders and down his chest. When she passed over his ribs, he hissed.

She gave him a sad look. "I'm sorry. I'm trying to be careful."

Going further south, her hands jerked to a stop and it was her turn to release a rush of air.

"I guess you weren't careful enough," he smirked.

Her wide-eyed gaze met his.

"I think I can finish from here." He didn't miss her gulp.

With a shaking hand she handed him the towel and left with the parting words, "There's a robe hanging on the back of the door."

Well, he'd won that standoff. Melanie wasn't as unaffected as she would like to make out. He let the towel drop to the floor. No way was he going to make the effort to put a robe on when he was just going to crawl into bed.

Melanie wasn't in the bedroom when he came out and he didn't pause on his way to the bed. The effort alone had his side aching. He managed to cover his lower half before there was a light knock on the door. He was in so much pain he didn't even make an effort to answer.

She pushed the door open enough to stick her head in. "You need help?"

He hated to admit again that he did. "Would you put some pillows behind me?"

Melanie hurried to him. She went around the bed, gathered the extra pillows and returned, placing the pillows within arm's reach.

Dalton groaned as he tried to sit up.

"Let me help you." Melanie didn't meet his look as she ran her left arm around his shoulders to support him. With her other hand, she stuffed a couple of pillows behind his back. The awkward process put them close. Too close for his comfort. His face was almost in her breasts. She smelled sweet. Nothing like the aroma of disinfectant their profession was known for. Too soon she guided him back against the pillows so that he was now in a half-sitting position. "Is that better?"

He nodded and made an effort to adjust the covers so that his reaction to her assistance wasn't obvious. Why was his body reacting to her so?

"Good. I'll get you that pain reliever." She stepped out of the room and soon returned with a bottle of tablets and a glass of water. Shaking out a couple of pills, she handed them to him, then offered him the glass of water.

Gladly he took the medicine and swallowed all the water. Closing his eyes, he was almost asleep when the covers were pulled up over his chest. He was being tucked in for the first time in his life…and he liked it!

CHAPTER THREE

MELANIE SETTLED IN to the overstuffed chair closest to the door to Dalton's bedroom. Dalton. She liked the name. He wasn't as much of a stuffed shirt when he was hurt. She would never have dreamed she would ever be babysitting the world's foremost orthopedic surgeon. Here she was spending the night and him really just a stranger. That might not be technically accurate after she'd toweled him dry. She'd been aware he was a man before, but she was well aware of how much man he was now.

Heavens, after those eventful moments in the bathroom she was almost glad he was hurt. She wasn't sure what she would have done had he leaned over and kissed her. Shaking her head, she tried to get the image out of her mind but it didn't seem to want to go. Being a professional, she shouldn't have been shocked or affected by his nakedness but somehow his body's reaction to her ministrations made her blood run hot. What was she thinking? She wasn't even sure she liked him. He'd made it clear he cared nothing about football and her life revolved around the game.

Her cell phone rang.

"Yes, Daddy?"

"How is Dr. Reynolds?"

Just like him not to ask about her. Tamping down her disappointment, she answered, "He's asleep and not too happy with having to be here longer than he planned."

"Well, try to keep him happy. We need him to sign off on Rocket."

"Dad, I wouldn't count on him doing that." Or her, for that matter. But that wasn't a battle she would have over the phone.

"Well, you never know. Since you're going to be spending some extra time with him, try to sweeten him up some."

That she *wouldn't* be doing. "I'll let you know if anything changes."

Her father hung up. She shifted to get more comfortable but that didn't seem to happen. Dalton might have taken the majority of the hit but she could tell that she hadn't escaped unhurt. She would like to sleep but she was waiting for one of the girls in the office to bring her some clothes.

While Dalton had showered, she'd called one of her friends and asked her to pack a bag and bring it by the Lodge. As soon as it arrived she would get a bath in the other room and then a nap.

As if thinking about it made it appear, there was a knock at the door. It was the bellhop with her bag. After thanking and tipping him, she closed and locked the door. She needed to check on Dalton before seeing to herself.

She set the bag on the floor next to Dalton's door and then pushed it open. It wouldn't pay for him to think she was sneaking a peek at him. She went to his bedside. He slept making a soft, even snoring sound. The covers had slipped down, leaving his chest bare. It was well developed as if he was used to physical activity. There was a smattering of hair in its center.

"Like what you see?"

Jerking back, heat rushing up her neck, her gaze flew to Dalton's face. "I was just checking on you."

"That's what they all say." His eyes closed again.

She left the room, hoping he wouldn't remember her visit.

* * *

A noise woke Melanie from where she slept on one of the sofas. She'd chosen to rest there so she could hear Dalton if she was needed. The extra bedroom was too far away.

She sat up. A fat ray of light came out of the open door. Dalton stood silhouetted in it. She sighed. At least he was wearing the robe.

"How're you feeling?"

"Hungry." His breathing still sounded difficult.

"I called for sandwiches earlier. They're in the refrigerator in the minibar. I'll get them." She stood. Pulling on the matching robe over her tailored-shirt-and-pants pajama set, she flipped on a lamp.

Giving her a critical look, he followed her to the bar. There he took one of the high stools. Melanie flipped on the light over the bar and pulled the tray of sandwiches out of the refrigerator, placing them on the bar. "What would you like to drink?"

Dalton glanced out the window. Following his gaze, she saw that the lamps lighting the falls made it easy to see snow falling.

He looked back at her. "Coffee?"

"Coming right up." She prepared the coffee machine and started it. While it bubbled and dripped she pulled out her own sandwich. "Cream and sugar?"

He shook his head.

"Does it still hurt to breathe?"

He nodded.

Pouring his coffee, she handed it to him. "Would you like more pain reliever?"

"Yes."

"I'll get you some after we eat." Despite his injury, she had a feeling he used as few words as possible all the time. She opened the refrigerator, pulled out a soda for herself and walked around the bar. Taking a stool, she made sure it wasn't the one right next to his.

They ate in silence. When Dalton finished he pushed the plate away and limped toward the window. He stood staring out. Melanie joined him. From this position the falls could be seen but it wasn't the same magnificent view as from his bedroom.

After a moment she murmured, "I want to thank you again for protecting me. I know getting stuck here wasn't what you planned."

"Not your fault."

"Still, I feel bad."

"Don't."

Neither one of them said anything for a few more minutes. Melanie was surprise by how comfortable it was to just stand next to him and look out at the snowy night. When was the last time she had spent a moment or two just being with someone?

Not that she was attracted to Dalton. She stepped away. "I need to clean up."

While she was busy behind the bar, Dalton went into his bedroom. Finished with putting everything in its place, Melanie went to Dalton's room to see about giving him some medicine. She found him sitting on the edge of the bed.

Melanie picked up the pain reliever bottle she'd left on the bedside table. Shaking out a couple of pills, she handed them to Dalton. She picked up the glass left there earlier. "I'll get you some water."

As she went by, his fingers circled her wrist, stopping her. His hand was warm on her skin. "Thank you for taking care of me."

Melanie could see the effort the words cost him, both physically and mentally. Had no one ever cared for him? Surely as a child his mother had nursed him when he was sick?

"I'm glad I could help."

He let go of her and she continued to the bathroom to

fill the glass. When she returned he was already asleep. The robe he'd worn lay on the end of the bed. He must have taken the pills dry. She left the glass on the table and adjusted the covers around his shoulders. After turning off the bedside lamp, she left the room, leaving the door cracked so she could hear him if he called.

Dalton woke to the sun streaming through the large window and the roar of the falls. He rolled over and let out a loud groan. He'd heard that having bruised or broken ribs was superpainful. What everyone said was right. If he had to sit up on a plane for three hours he wouldn't be fit to do anything for a week. Thankfully, he didn't have any cases waiting. He looked at the snow piled on the windowsill and shivered. Cold was just not his thing.

The door opened and Melanie's head appeared around it. "You okay in here? I heard you call out."

"Yes."

"You hungry again?"

He nodded. "What time is it?"

"Almost eleven."

"That late?" When was the last time he'd not been up at six?

Melanie glanced out the window. "How about some hot cereal?"

"Okay."

"Cream of Wheat okay?"

He'd not had Cream of Wheat in years. Mrs. Richie had served it almost every morning. It was a cheap way to feed a large number of children. The thing was, he didn't really mind. He, unlike most of the other children, liked the cereal.

"Sounds good."

"You seem to be breathing easier. Has some of the pain gone away?"

He shrugged. "Not really."

"I'm sorry to hear that. I'll call for some breakfast." She left, pulling the door closed.

Dalton struggled to stand. The pain was excruciating, but he couldn't lie there all day. That certainly wouldn't make it any easier to get around. He also didn't want Melanie to come back and start helping him dress. If she saw him in the nude again it had better be for his benefit as well as hers. *Damn*, where did that thought come from?

He had no interest in Melanie. Then again, he was stuck here for a few days. He had time to kill and he was attracted to her. But they really had nothing in common outside of their profession. Last night had been a normal male reaction to a woman toweling him dry and nothing more.

With great effort and teeth-gritting pain, he managed to get his clothes on. He was grateful for his loafers because those he could at least slip his feet into, even if they were inadequate for the weather.

He joined Melanie in the living area. She was dressed in another well-cut suit. The only concession to her being a woman was the ruffles down the front of her shirt.

There was a knock at the door and she went to answer it. The bellhop pushed a cart in. Melanie smiled and called him by name. How like her to have made a friend. Dalton thought how it had taken years for him to cultivate the friends he had.

After tipping the bellhop, she closed the door, then pushed the cart toward the bar area. "I thought you might like a real pot of coffee and maybe some eggs with the cereal."

"That sounds good."

She started setting food on the bar. He went to help and she said, "No. I'll get it. You're still not in very good shape."

"I need to move some or I'll get so stiff that I can't." He took the same stool as he had the night before.

"Give it a few more hours before you start getting too energetic." She poured a cup of coffee from a carafe and placed it in front of him.

"You do remember I'm a doctor?"

"I do. And I'm one too, well aware of the kind of care you need. I also feel very responsible for what happened to you. So please humor me for a little while longer." She set the food out and removed the covers. "You'll be on your own soon enough."

"How's that?"

She joined him, taking what he now considered her stool. "I work at the local hospital one day a week and today is that day."

"Really?"

"Yes, really."

He picked up his spoon. "It's just that I'm a little surprised. So you're going to trust me here by myself?"

"I think your ribs will keep you in line."

He looked out the window. The idea of being stuck in the suite all day by himself with nothing to do might be more painful than trying to breathe.

"Mind if I tag along?"

Melanie viewed at him as if he were a bug under a magnifying glass. Was he not welcome? "You want to go to the hospital with me?"

"I think it'll be a pretty long day if I stay here."

"Are you sure you feel up to it?"

"I'll make it." He took a sip of his coffee. "I'll have pain pills."

"Okay. If that's what you want to do."

Half an hour later they were getting their coats on. Melanie stepped over and helped him pull his collar up around his neck when he couldn't bring himself to attempt it. Melanie seemed to know he needed assistance without him asking. She was no doubt a caring and thoughtful doctor. Somehow it was getting easier to accept her help. "Thanks."

She smiled and headed toward the door. "If you stay around much longer you're going to have to buy some clothes or you'll freeze to death."

Dalton huffed, which brought on a stab of pain. "Would we have time to stop somewhere before going to the hospital?"

She opened the suite door. "No, but we can afterwards."

Her eagerness to get to the hospital intrigued him. The fact she made a point to work at a hospital each week was interesting. There was more to Dr. Hyde than met the eye.

The same driver who had brought them to the hospital was waiting on them in front of the Lodge. He drove them to Melanie's car at the Currents' complex. It had been sitting outside and she removed snow from the windshield before leaving. The inside of the car was so cold it seemed to never warm up. Dalton could hardly wait to buy some heavier clothes.

Melanie wasn't sure that bringing Dalton along to the hospital was such a good idea, but she didn't have the heart to leave him alone all day. Even if she had to have a shadow, it was better than leaving him behind. She'd had no idea that her assignment to pick him up at the airport would lead to her entertaining him for days.

"So where do you work when you go to the hospital?" Dalton asked.

"In the peds department."

"Wow, that's a big difference from working with the team."

"Not really. Both come in with stomachaches and injuries. The size is the only difference."

"I guess you're right."

They entered the Niagara Hospital through a staff door near the Emergency Department. Melanie loved the old stone building. There was nothing chrome and glass about it, yet it offered state-of-the-art medical care. She enjoyed her work with the Currents, but her heart was with the kids.

Heat immediately hit her in the face and Melanie started removing her outer clothes. Dalton unbuttoned his thin overcoat. She continued along the corridor to the end where the service elevator was located and he followed. As they started upward, she said, "This hospital cares for about seventy-five percent poverty level patients. Most can't pay outside of government assistance. Many only come in after they have no choice because their problem is so bad."

Dalton looked at her. "So how does the hospital stay open?"

"By support of the people who live around here and fund-raising. The Currents do a fund-raiser in the off-season each year. A get-to-spend-the-day-with-a-pro-player type of event."

The elevator door opened and they stepped out.

Dalton asked, "Is it successful?"

"Very. People come from all over the world to see their favorite player. Rocket earned the most in the bidding last year." Melanie turned to the left and walked down the wide hallway. She went by the patient rooms and stopped at the nurses' station. All the while she was conscious of Dalton beside her. He would be taking in the place with percep-tive eyes. She'd seen his intense evaluation of Rocket and had no doubt he would do the same here.

The clerk sitting behind the desk said, "Good morning, Dr. Hyde. Marcus has been asking for you."

Mel chuckled. "I'm sure he's looking for a piece of candy. I'll start my rounds with him.

"Lisa, this is Dr. Reynolds. He's going to be doing rounds with me today."

Lisa gave Dalton a curious look. "Nice to meet you, Doctor."

Dalton nodded. Melanie was confident he was out of his medical element. She'd seen pictures of his shiny new clinic set in the South Beach area of Miami. No doubt he would have a hard time identifying with the type of patients this hospital typically saw.

"Well, I guess I better get started since Marcus has been looking for me." She turned and headed along another short hall. Over her shoulder she said to Dalton, "We can leave our coats in an office down here."

A few minutes later Melanie knocked on Marcus's room door and pushed it open.

"Dr. Mel!" The eleven-year-old boy had big eyes and a wide smile.

"Hi there, Marcus." She walked to the bedside and Dalton came to stand at the end. "How're you feeling today?"

"Pretty good. Are the Currents ready for the game on Sunday?"

Melanie looked at Dalton. "This guy is a walking encyclopedia of Currents statistics."

"That's impressive." Dalton sounded sincere despite his disinterest in football. She appreciated him being positive for the boy.

"This is Dr. Reynolds, Marcus. He's helping me out today."

The boy looked at Dalton. "Hi, Doc. You like the Currents?"

Dalton shrugged. "I did meet Rocket Overtree yesterday. He seemed like a nice guy."

Marcus lit up like a Christmas tree and started asking questions at a rapid pace.

Finally Melanie held up a hand. "I think that's enough questions. I need to check you out."

"Aw, come on, Dr. Mel. I want to hear about Rocket."

Dalton smiled. "We should let Dr. Mel do her thing. She might be feeling left out."

Melanie gave him an appreciative look and pulled her stethoscope from around her neck. "Okay, let me give you a listen."

Marcus swung his legs around to sit on the edge of the bed.

Melanie leaned toward him. "Heart first."

"Dr. Mel, I know the drill by now." Exasperation filled Marcus's voice.

She smiled. "I guess you do."

Melanie always hoped when she put her stethoscope to the boy's chest she wouldn't hear the swish and gurgle that said he had a bad valve. Marcus's family couldn't afford the medical care he needed. To her great disappointment, the sounds were just as strong as ever.

"Okay, deep breath time." She moved her stethoscope to his back.

Marcus filled his lungs and released them a couple of times.

"Well, you sound good," she lied. He did for someone in need of heart surgery. With every week that went by he was getting weaker.

Dalton moved to stand beside Melanie. "Marcus, do you mind if I listen to you also?"

"Sure. If you want to."

"Mind?" He indicated her stethoscope.

Pleasantly surprised that he was showing this much interest in Marcus, Melanie handed the instrument to him. She'd figured all he would do was follow her around killing time and have no direct interaction with her patients. Since his specialty was adult medicine, she'd thought he'd have no interest. Her primary practice had to do with grown men but she looked forward to the one day she spent on the pediatric floor. Difference was that he'd probably had the opportunity to choose his area of medicine while she had been told she would be a team doctor.

Melanie watched Dalton's face. His mouth tightened. He must have heard what she did. Dalton looked at her with concern showing in his eyes.

"Thanks, Marcus." Dalton handed the stethoscope back to her.

Melanie took it and wrapped it around her neck. To Marcus she said, "I'll stop by before I leave today. I forgot I have something for you. I left it in the office."

"Okay. But don't forget."

Melanie laughed. "I won't."

"I won't let her," Dalton added with a smile as he followed her out. When the door was closed between them and Marcus, Dalton demanded, "Why hasn't he had surgery?"

"Because his parents can't afford it. A couple of doctors are getting together to try to work something out. Have him moved to a children's hospital and find some financing."

"He's not going to be able to wait long."

She glared at him and worked to keep her voice even. "Don't you think I know that? I've been seeing him on and off for months. I'm well aware of how far the damage has progressed."

His expression turned contrite. "I'm used to fixing problems right away. I didn't mean to imply that you weren't doing all you could."

Was that his way of saying he was sorry? "I might have overreacted. I know we aren't supposed to have favorites, but Marcus is mine."

"That's understandable. He's a nice kid. Seems smart too."

She walked down the hall to the next room. "He's managed to have excellent grades despite being in and out of here."

"So who do we see next?" Dalton asked.

Over the next hour they fell into the routine of stopping outside the room door of the next patient while Melanie gave him a brief medical history. They saw children from two to eighteen years of age.

Only a couple of times did Dalton wince when he made a move, otherwise Melanie would have never known he'd been injured. The man sure could hold his emotions in check.

"This is our last stop. Josey Woods is a teen who has just finished chemo. She's made good progress but has pneumonia. She was admitted for a little support since she couldn't seem to shake it on her own. If all goes well she'll be going home tomorrow."

Dalton nodded and they entered the room. A young girl sat in a chair watching a music video on the TV hanging on the wall. There was a blanket lying across her legs.

"Hello, Josey. I'm Dr. Mel Hyde. You can call me Dr. Mel and this is Dr. Reynolds. We're going to be checking on you today."

"Hi," Josey said softly, not making eye contact. Blond fuzz covered her bald head.

"I hear you're feeling better and ready to go home." Melanie stepped closer.

The girl nodded.

Dalton hung back near the door. Apparently he was sensitive to the shy patient, whose mannerisms indicated she might have "white coat syndrome." Melanie was glad that neither she nor Dalton were wearing their lab jackets.

"I'd like to listen to you, if I may?" Melanie asked.

Josey leaned forward as if she was resigned to having no choice. She, like Marcus, had been in the hospital for far too much of her childhood.

"I see you like Taylor Swift," Melanie said as she prepared to place the stethoscope on Josey's thin chest.

"Yes, she's my favorite."

"I like her music too." Melanie listened to the steady thump, thump, thump of her heart. It sounded good.

"You do?" Josey seemed to perk up. She leaned forward.

"I do. Take a deep breath." Melanie glanced to where Dalton leaned against the wall just inside the closed door. He had a slight smile on his face.

Josey eagerly announced, "I have her autograph."

"You do? Another breath. I'd love to see it."

A few seconds later Josey said, "I'll show it to you." She pushed the blanket off her legs and rose. Dressed in a long-sleeve T-shirt and flannel pants, she moved around the bed. There was a limp to her stride. She took a glossy photo off the bed tray and came back to Melanie, handing it to her.

"I'm so jealous." Melanie smiled at the girl and handed the picture back.

"Taylor is too girly for me. I'm a bigger fan of CeeLo Green," Dalton said, having stepped toward them.

Josey looked at him. "I like him too."

"I'd bet you like Justin Timberlake too." Dalton's voice held a teasing note.

Josey's cheeks turned pink. "Yes. I like his music."

Dalton looked from first Josey to Melanie. "All the women I know like his looks."

"Hey, don't pull me into this conversation," Melanie protested.

Dalton came to stand beside her. To Josey he said, "Would you mind if I looked at your legs?"

She acted unsure but then she said, "I guess that would be okay. I've been told there's nothing that can be done about them."

"I'd just like to look. I promise not to hurt you."

Melanie had to give him kudos for his bedside manner with the girl. He'd found common ground before he approached the skittish patient. The man had skill.

"Josey, would you please walk to the door and back this way for me?"

She nodded and did as he asked.

When she returned Dalton said, "Please sit on the edge of your bed. I'm going to feel your legs. If at any time you are uncomfortable let me know and I'll stop."

"Okay."

Dalton went down on his heels. He felt her feet and moved along one leg and then the other. The look on his face was the same one he'd worn when he examined Rocket. Dalton used his fingers to tell him what he needed to know. A few minutes later he stood.

"I'm sorry to have to ask you this but I need you to remove your socks and pants so I can see your knees. If you have some shorts to put on that would be fine."

Josey looked at Melanie, who gave the girl a reassuring smile.

"Okay."

"We'll step out into the hall. Just call when you're ready." He started toward the door and Melanie followed.

She closed the door behind them. "I had no idea about her limp. It wasn't on the chart."

"My guess is that she and her family have just accepted it."

A faint, "I'm ready," came from inside the room.

Dalton went in ahead of Melanie this time. He was in his element and seemed eager to see if something could be done for Josey, who was already sitting on the side of the bed with the sheet pulled over her waist.

"I'm ready."

"Great. I'm going to do something similar to what I've already done. All you have to do is sit there. If what I do hurts, just let me know."

Dalton put his hands on her right knee and manipulated it. He then moved to the left, the one with the limp. A few minutes later he stood and backed away. "I'd like to look at your left hip. All you have to do is lie on the bed and let me move your leg back and forth. You can tell me 'no' and I'll understand."

"Okay."

Just like a teen, she used only one-word answers.

Josey scooted back on the bed, lay down and adjusted the sheet. Melanie worked to control her smile. A girl was modest at that age, even around a male doctor. Melanie looked at Dalton. Especially one as good-looking as him. She couldn't blame Josey. She'd have felt much the same way if she was half-clothed in front of Dalton.

"I'm going to raise your leg up. Tell me when I've gone as far as I can." He lifted her leg slowly.

Thankfully the range of movement looked fine.

He brought the leg out to the left and then across her other leg. "Good. You can sit up." He offered his hand to Josey. She took it and he pulled her upright. "I'm glad you are doing so well and getting to go home tomorrow."

"Me too."

"We'll let you get back to your videos," Melanie said as she followed Dalton out the door as the sound of a popular song on the TV grew.

Dalton stopped when they were well out of hearing distance from anyone who might be in the hall. "I would like to see X-rays of her knee, both front and side view. I would also like to see the MRI."

"I doubt either have been done."

"You have to be kidding. Why not?" He paced three steps up the hall then turned and came back to her.

"Because there was no reason to. She is being treated for an infection as a complication to chemo. There would be no reason either should have been ordered. Here—" she gestured around her at the building "—we are treating her cancer issues. The leg issues were not on the staff radar."

His sound of disgust rubbed her the wrong way. She wasn't to blame here. If it were up to her these children would all have the finest medical care money could buy. For people like Josey and her parents it was an everyday worry about how they would pay for Josey's needs.

"Then they should be ordered," Dalton said sharply.

Now he was starting to tell her what to do. "That's easier said than done."

He glared at her. "Why is that?"

"The X-rays are doable but the MRI is a problem."

He stepped forward, his frustration written all over his face. "And I ask again—why is that?"

"Because there is no MRI machine here. She would need to be transferred to another hospital to have it done."

"Then do it."

She pulled him into an empty patient room. "Now wait a minute. You don't give me orders. You're not even on the staff here. So don't start throwing your ego around!"

Dalton looked at her calmly but the tic in his jaw gave his irritation away. "You don't want to help the girl?"

Melanie stepped back as if she had been slapped. "Of course I do."

"Okay, then. The first step is seeing that we get X-rays of her knee and a MRI if possible."

"I can order an X-ray. I'll have to see how best to proceed with the MRI."

"Good. Let's go do it."

When she didn't move Dalton took her elbow and gave her a little nudge.

Melanie pulled her arm out of his grip. Head held high, she walked down the hall. Had she ever been this angry? Who did he think he was, telling her what to do? Making demands. And, worse, implying she didn't care enough to do everything that could be done for Josey.

Stalking to the nurse's station, she went to one of the computer stations and typed in her password. She pulled up Josey's chart and ordered an X-ray with anteroposterior and lateral views.

"I'd like a skyline as well."

She looked up. Her face was inches from his. Dalton's arms were braced on the back of her chair as he leaned over her, looking at the screen.

She snapped, "You do understand that you don't have privilege at this hospital?"

"That's why I'm asking you to request one."

"Request? I missed that part." She was starting to sound childish even to her own ears. Thankfully no one was in the charting room to overhear.

Dalton sat in the empty chair next to her. He grunted as he did so, which reminded her that he still hurt. "Look, I'm sorry if I sound as if I'm telling you what to do, it's just that I think I can help Josey. Sometimes I get high-handed in my excitement." His fingertips touched her arm for a second. "Would you please also request a skyline view?"

She wasn't sure she liked his manipulation any better than being told what to do. What she did appreciate was his passion about helping Josey. He saw a problem, believed he could fix it and wouldn't stop until he tried. If only all that just didn't come with his general barking-orders attitude.

She gave him a sideways look intended to show him that she knew he was managing her, then typed in the order.

"When should those be back?" Dalton asked, standing.

"Tomorrow at the earliest. They are not a priority, so she won't have them done until morning." When he started to say something, she put up a hand to stop him. "You will just have to accept that. I will not push anymore."

"If I get a flight out tomorrow will you see they are sent to me?"

Melanie pushed away from the computer. "I will. Despite what you might think, I'd like to see Josey walk without a limp."

A heart-melting smile came to his face. "I never thought any different."

"You sure implied it."

"How about I buy you dinner tonight to make up for that?"

Melanie met his gaze. "Now you are using bribery to get your way."

He shrugged. "You have to eat, don't you?"

She did, but not necessarily with him.

"So what's next?" Dalton asked.

"I have to do some dictation. See that charts are up to date."

He groaned. "I think I'll find the cafeteria and get a bad cup of coffee. That sounds like more fun."

It hadn't been as uncomfortable as she'd anticipated to have Dalton around but it was nice to have a few minutes to herself.

For the next few hours Melanie worked her way through the charting and made sure orders were posted. While she did so she overheard a number of the nurses talking to each other about Dalton. More than once a comment was made about how good-looking he was, followed by the question of whether or not he was married, then giggles. If they knew what a stuffed shirt he was, how demanding he could be, or that he hated sports and snow, they might not have been so impressed.

But he had been chivalrous when he protected her from getting hit, had been fair with Rocket and almost warrior-like with Josey. Maybe there was something more socially redeeming in him than she cared to admit.

She hadn't seen Dalton since he'd left for coffee. Where had he gotten to? Great, now she'd have to go hunt him down. Melanie glanced at the computer. Marcus's chart was still up. Before leaving she needed to go by and give him his present.

Returning to the office where she and Dalton had left their coats, she looked through her pocketbook and pulled out the tickets to the Currents' Sunday afternoon playoff game. She went down the hall and stopped at Marcus's door. The music from what sounded like an adventure movie came from inside the room. She knocked and received no answer. That didn't surprise her. Pushing the door open just far enough to call Marcus, she waited for an answer and heard none.

"Man, that's the best. Luke made him pay," Marcus's voice carried.

"Darth Vader is a villain's villain."

That was Dalton. Even in a few short days she had his voice committed to memory.

Melanie pushed the door open to find Marcus sitting up in bed and Dalton reclined in a chair next to him. Flashing on the TV was a Star Wars movie. A loud swish and boom filled the air. Neither male gave her any notice as she walked farther into the room.

"What's going—?"

"Shh, this is the best part," Dalton said, not even bothering to look her way.

Melanie moved around behind him and regarded the screen. Two people using light sabers slashed at one another.

Marcus leaned forward. "Wow, look at how he makes that move."

Obviously the two males had found something to bond over. She didn't say anything again until the fight was over. Even then she spoke softly to Dalton. "I'm ready to head out when you are."

He glanced at her. "This is almost over."

From that statement he left no doubt he wasn't leaving until then. Against the wall on the other side of the room was an extra hardback chair. She circled the bed toward it. Dalton and Marcus both groaned as she walked between them and the TV.

"Aw, come on, Dr. Mel," Marcus whined as he put his head one way then the other to see around her.

"Hurry up, Dr. Hyde." Dalton shifted in much the same manner as Marcus had.

She hurried by them. While pulling the chair in the direction of the bed, it made a scraping noise on the floor. Both movie watchers glared at her for a second before they returned to viewing the action.

"Sorry," she said contritely before picking up the chair. She placed it on the floor next to Marcus's bed and primly sat on it. Did she dare disturb them?

Less than half an hour later the movie ended.

"No matter how many times I see it, it's great. A classic." Dalton stood with effort and a slight grimace.

"You're right, bro, one of the best movies ever." Marcus brought his legs to the floor.

Melanie looked from one of them to the other. "Who are you two?"

"We're Star Wars fans." Marcus acted as if that was a badge of honor that had bonded him and Dalton together forever.

She nodded as if she understood what that meant. "Well, it's time for Dr. Reynolds and me to go. I just came down to bring you what I promised. It's not a trip to a Star Wars convention so I hope you still like it."

Marcus looked at her eagerly. "What is it?"

"How about box tickets to the Currents' play-off game on Sunday?"

His huge white smile stood out in contrast to his dark skin. "Man, really? Box seats! How cool."

His smile suddenly faded.

"What's wrong?" Melanie asked.

"I'm stuck in here." He looked at his bed.

"I fixed that too. You have a pass out for the day as long as you do exactly what you're told."

Marcus's smile grew again. "You can count on that." He turned to Dalton. "Will you be there?"

"No, I'll be leaving before then. But I'm sure you'll have fun."

"I can't wait. I just hope 'The Rocket' will play."

Melanie looked at Dalton, then said, "We'll have to see about that. There'll be a car here to pick you up on Sunday. You can bring one person with you. I'll stop in and say hi when you get to the stadium."

"Thanks, Dr. Mel. You rock."

"You're welcome. See you then." Melanie turned toward the door.

"It was nice to meet you, Marcus. I hope you're out of here soon." Dalton offered his hand.

Marcus placed his thin one in Dalton's and they shook.

"Later, man." Marcus put large headphones over his ears and picked up an iPad.

"That was a nice thing you did for Marcus," Dalton said.

Melanie shrugged. "No big deal. They were offered to me and I gave them to him."

"I have the feeling that you do whatever you can to make these kids happy. You have a big heart, Melanie."

She had to admit it give her a warm feeling to have him notice how much she cared. Her family wasn't even aware of where she spent her days off. She'd let this stranger into her world without even thinking. Even so, she didn't plan to let him too close—she'd seen what happened when she allowed that. Her work with the kids was her private domain.

Why had she shared it with him?

CHAPTER FOUR

IN THE PASSENGER seat of Melanie's car as they left the hospital parking lot, Dalton asked, "Where're we headed now?"

"I thought the mall might give us the most choices for men's shops." She looked over and grinned. "I didn't think you'd want to get out in the weather any more than necessary. At least in the mall it'll be warm between stores."

"You're enjoying my discomfort."

She glanced at him with a grin on her lips. "Enjoy may be too strong a word. It's more like I find it humorous."

Dalton watched as her grin transformed into a smile. Melanie's lips were full, with a curve on each end as if they were always waiting to lift in pleasure. What would it feel like to kiss them? Would they be as plush as they looked? He'd see to it she smiled with pleasure.

Where had those thoughts come from? He shifted in his seat. No doubt it came from the attraction he felt for her. "What's so entertaining about it?"

"That a man of your intelligence would come this far north in the middle of winter without the correct type of clothes."

He smirked and chuckled. "You're right. Put that way, I don't sound too smart. My only defense is that I hadn't planned to stay so long."

They both laughed. Snow continued to fall and the

traffic increased. He sat in silence as Melanie concentrated on driving.

"I hope you weren't too bored today." Melanie pulled out into the traffic along the major freeway.

"No, it was fine." Dalton hadn't spent a more satisfying day in a long time. Despite the fact that his whole body hurt, he had enjoyed working with the children and seeing different medical issues. He'd spent so long in the adult-care world, and focused on bones and tissue, it was refreshing to think small and broader.

He'd found out he and Melanie shared a common interest in children. That had come as a surprise. She kept doing that. First she was a female team doctor working in the NFL. Melanie also wasn't easily deterred from what she believed was her duty, which showed in her insisting she take care of him. And now he'd found out her real love was children. He'd never met a more fascinating woman with such diverse interests. It would be exciting to discover other aspects of her personality. At least while he was stuck there.

They hadn't traveled far when Melanie exited the freeway. She drove down a side road and turned into the parking area of a shopping mall. The lot was full and they rode up and down the aisles looking for a spot. "People are out Christmas shopping. With only six days left, the mall is packed."

"You don't Christmas shop?" He understood that women lived to shop.

"I did mine months ago. I don't like to wait to the last minute."

"I'm impressed."

Melanie turned to him. "So how about you? Do you have all your shopping done? Do you need to do some while we are here?"

What should he tell her? He didn't have anyone to buy for? "My secretary handles that for me."

She glanced at him. "Really?"

Dalton chose to ignore the question in the hope she wouldn't pursue it.

She found a parking spot about as far away from the entrance as possible. He wasn't looking forward to the frigid walk. The sun was setting and the temperature dropping. Bundling up as best he could, he started across the parking lot beside Melanie.

"I should have dropped you off at the door and then parked," she said apologetically.

"I wouldn't have allowed you to walk across this large lot by yourself." He stuffed his hands in his pockets as the wind picked up. "Not safe."

"Your mother must have taught you to be a gentleman."

Despite all the years that had passed, his chest tightened. He let her push through the revolving door first and then followed in the next partition. He said, more to himself than her, "No, that's one thing she wasn't guilty of."

"There's a men's shop down here on the right that should have what you need. I'm sorry you're having to buy clothes you won't have much use for later."

"It's better than being in the hospital for frostbite. Besides, I'm sure this won't be my only trip up north."

"Well, there is that." Melanie headed into the mall and he fell into step beside her.

They walked past the glass-fronted stores and around the next corner.

"I love to come here during the holidays. The decorations always put me in the holiday spirit." Enthusiasm filled her voice.

"I've never really thought about it."

She pointed up. "Where in the world can you see ornaments larger than a person? Or such beautiful trees?"

The wonder in her voice was almost contagious.

"You said you always have your shopping done early. Does that mean you just come to the mall to get in the middle of thousands of people because you like the decorations?"

"I do. As long as I don't have to fight over gifts I like being in the middle of things."

"Then I'll make sure I hold you back while I'm trying to buy clothes. I wouldn't want you to get in a scuffle."

She laughed. "Thanks, I'd appreciate that. I wouldn't want to reflect poorly on the Currents' name."

"Do you always think about the team first?"

She shrugged. "I guess that's how I was raised."

"It seems to me you should think about yourself first every once in a while. I've not known you long, but you're quite a unique person. There's a lot more to you than your work with the team."

Melanie stopped walking to look at him. "Thank you—that was nice of you to say."

Her admiration made him uncomfortable. "Don't sound so surprised. I can be nice."

"Here's the shop I told you about. I think you'll find what you need in here."

"You're not coming in? What if I don't get the right stuff?"

"I was just going to wait out here for you, but if you'd like my help…"

"I could use it." He could decide on his own clothes but he enjoyed seeing her flustered. He liked teasing her and he never teased.

"Okay."

He went through the open doors of the store and she followed.

Dalton looked around. "So what do you recommend?"

She said without hesitation, "You need a couple of flannel shirts, heavy sweater, cord slacks and thick socks."

"Wow, I'm almost sorry I asked."

"You really should have a jacket but, since you aren't going to be here long, I hate for you to spend that kind of money. Especially when you might not wear it again anytime soon."

"Can I help you?" a blonde saleswoman wearing a tight dress and a smile asked.

"Yes. I'm interested in a couple of warm slacks, two shirts and a sweater."

Her smile grew. "Well, you're in the correct place. Come right this way."

Dalton glanced at Melanie and caught her rolling her eyes. She didn't seem impressed with his reception. Interesting.

Melanie tagged along behind Dalton as he followed Miss Fresh and Perky toward the back of the store. He seemed more than willing. Why it mattered to her, she had no idea.

"Right, here is our slacks selection." The clerk waved a hand toward a rack of pants, then pulled a pair out. "I think these would look great on you. I'm guessing a thirty-four/thirty-four."

Dalton nodded and smiled as if she'd given him a compliment.

No wonder her brothers said this was their favorite place to shop.

Dalton felt the material. He looked at her. "What do you think?"

Melanie was surprised he remembered she was there. She stepped forward and rubbed the pants leg. "They should do."

"Why don't you try them on so your wife can see them?" the saleswoman said.

"She's not my wife," Dalton said.

At the same time Melanie said, "I'm not his wife."

The saleswoman's smile brightened. "I'm sorry. My mistake. The dressing rooms are this way."

"Melanie, while I'm trying these on, would you mind picking out some shirts? A sweater, if you see one you like," Dalton called over his shoulder; he seemed far too eager to follow the saleswoman.

If Melanie didn't know better she would say she was feeling jealous. That wasn't something she made a habit of. Why would she care if a saleswoman flirted with Dalton? He was nothing to her. Still, he knew more about her than her own family.

She walked to the other side of the store to where the shirts hung and picked out a couple that would look nice on Dalton. Nearby on a shelf was a stack of sweaters in multiple colors. She pulled out one in burgundy and held it up. With Dalton's coloring it would suit him. Making her way back to where Dalton stood talking to the saleswoman, she joined them. They were both laughing.

"I found these. Do you want to try them on?" she said in a sharper than normal tone.

With a raised brow, Dalton asked, "What size are they?"

She told him.

"Those will do. How about a sweater?"

Melanie held it out for him to see.

"That color is perfect for you," the saleswoman cooed.

"Then I'll take it." He grinned at Melanie.

She'd had all she could take. This obvious flirtation was starting to make her sick. Why it mattered Melanie couldn't fathom, but it did. Outside of that one time in the bathroom when he'd handed her the towel, he'd treated her like a colleague. But wasn't that what she was? Why did she want him to flirt with her the same way?

Because it would be nice to feel like a woman. In her world, both at work and with her family, she was treated like one of the boys. Was she guilty of letting them do so?

The saleswoman took the clothes. "Is there anything else I can get you?"

Dalton's far-too-syrupy grin had Melanie walking off. "I think you can handle the rest without me."

Fifteen minutes later Dalton exited the store. Melanie

sat on a bench in the middle of the mall, waiting. When he joined her, she said, "You seemed to be enjoying your shopping trip."

He grinned. "I was. What about a coat?"

"If you really want one there's a store down this way." She stood and started walking down the mall. "It carries a good line of coats. There may not be a salesperson in a tight dress, though."

"Do I hear a touch of jealousy in there?"

"You do not. I just don't think clerks have to wear skin-tight clothes to sell men's clothing."

"What should she wear? Something functional like your suits?"

"What's wrong with my suits? They're businesslike. Professional looking." She raised her voice.

"I think you can be professional and look like a woman too."

She turned to him. "Are you saying I don't?" Her anger grew. People were beginning to look.

"You can dress anyway you wish."

"You're right—it's none of your business." Melanie stalked ahead of him.

By the time he had reached her side, they had arrived at the coat store.

"I don't think you'll need my help here. I'm going to look next door. I'll meet you right here when you're finished."

Melanie didn't give Dalton time to answer before she walked on. She needed to get away from him for a few minutes. Stopping at the show window, she looked at the mannequins dressed in glitzy dresses in seasonal colors. Did she really dress unfemininely? Here she was, carting him around, seeing he had warm clothes, and he was giving her fashion advice. How much nerve could the man have?

She looked down at her high-quality tailored suit. These

were the kind of clothes she'd always worn. That wasn't true. Her mother had dressed her in frilly dresses, especially on holidays.

When her mom died, her father had spent little time worrying about how Melanie dressed. He'd handed money over to the housekeeper or babysitters and asked them to buy her clothing for special occasions. As she grew older her father gave the money to her. Melanie was a tomboy and that was encouraged. She looked up to her brothers, so she tended to choose shirts and jeans to wear like them.

For the prom, her friend's mother had taken her and her friend to buy their dresses. It was one of the few times she had female help with picking out clothing or with any of the other rites of passage most girls shared with their mother. A few times she'd cried herself to sleep when she heard about events like a Mother/Daughter Luncheon or when her friends talked about spending a day shopping with their mothers. She had long ago moved past feeling sorry for herself and compensated by making herself needed by her father and brothers. That was where she found her security. It would be wonderful to feel appreciated, just the same.

Why had Dalton's one comment got under her skin? Had she forgotten how to dress like a girl? Had she been living in the world of men so long that she'd given up even trying to act like a woman? When was the last time she'd bought something lacy and girly? She did like sexy underwear but few had seen that side of her.

"So which one do you like best?" Dalton's deep voice said beside her.

She jerked around. He'd caught her looking at the dresses. Now he would be pleased that what he'd said had got to her. To cover her embarrassment, she asked, "Did you find a coat?"

"You answer my question, then I'll answer yours."

She huffed. The man exasperated her. "The red one, if you must know."

The dress was mid-thigh-length and had a scooped neck. It fit tightly down to the waist then flared out into a full skirt. She'd seen fewer dresses prettier.

"Are you going to try it on?"

"You haven't answered my question."

Dalton held up a sack. "I did get a coat. I bought it on sale so you don't have to worry about me spending so much money. So are you going in?"

"No. I don't need a dress like that."

He seemed to give that remark some thought, then looked at her. "Shame. I think you'd look very pretty in it."

Melanie didn't want to admit the glow of warmth his words created.

As if he'd forgotten what they had been talking about, he said, "Hey, I'm hungry. Is there a decent restaurant here?"

"There's one down the next wing."

They made their way through the growing crowd to the restaurant. In front of the brick-facade pub, they stopped and he gave the girl standing behind a podium his name.

"Why don't we wait at the bar?" Dalton suggested.

Melanie nodded.

They took stools next to each other.

"Would you like a drink?" Dalton asked.

She ordered wine and he a whiskey.

"I haven't asked in a while, but how are you feeling?" Melanie fingered the stem of her glass.

"Let's just say that I know where my ribs are located."

"Maybe you should have stayed at the Lodge and rested."

"Are you kidding? If I had done that I wouldn't be moving now. How about you? Feeling any aftereffects?"

"When I turn a certain way I know something has happened."

Dalton nodded.

The hostess approached and said their table was ready.

Dalton placed his hand at her waist as she slid off the high stool. His fingers were warm and firm but soon fell away. She was far too aware of him following her as they maneuvered between the tables, trailing the hostess, carrying their drinks with them.

The girl seated them beside the roaring fire in the center of the dining area. The table was covered in a white cloth and a small lantern burned in the center. It was far too romantic a setting for Melanie's comfort.

"Is this table okay with you?" Dalton asked.

"Uh, sure."

"You don't sound very confident."

The man was perceptive. She'd have to watch her facial expressions around him. "No, no, it's fine."

Dalton helped her with her chair, then took the one beside her, facing the fire. His knee touched hers under the table and she shifted away.

"You have enough room?"

"I'm fine."

"I have a feeling you've said that most of your life." He picked up the menu that the hostess had left on the table.

What did he mean by that statement?

Dalton flipped through the menu. "Have you ever eaten here? Do you know what's good?"

"I've had lunch a few times. I always have either a salad or burger. So I'm not much help on the other stuff."

"I want something warm. Go-down-into-the-bones warm."

She grinned. "Now that you have clothes you're going to feel much better."

"I'm counting on that. I going to start with some soup and have a steak. How about you?"

"I'm going to have a salad and roasted chicken."

When the waitress came, Dalton gave her their order.

Dalton had been asking her questions regularly and Melanie was determined to take advantage of this time to ask a few of her own.

"So tell me, why did you become an orthopedic doctor?"

He took a sip of his drink, then placed the glass carefully on the table. Did it make him uncomfortable to answer personal questions? He certainly didn't seem to mind asking them.

"I was a good student. I took a biology class and was hooked on science. Medicine just seemed like the natural progression."

"So why orthopedics?"

"When I did that rotation, there was this man who had been crippled for most of his life. He agreed to a new procedure and now he's walking. I wanted to make that possible for people."

That answer she liked. She was glad to know he hadn't got into it for the money. With his fancy practice, she'd wondered what motivated him.

He continued, "I have a talent for what I do. The next thing I knew, I was being asked to evaluate athletes. One thing led to another."

"Seems like you have a high-pressure practice."

"It can be but I have a great staff and a couple of other doctors working with me."

"So what do you do to blow off steam when it gets to be too much?"

"Why, Melanie, are you trying to find out about my private life?" There he was with the uncomfortable questions again.

"I am not. I'm trying to have pleasant conversation over dinner."

Dalton's hand came to rest over hers for a second. "It's pleasant being here with you."

"I think you're trying to dodge the question."

Grinning, he nodded. "Maybe a little. I'm a pretty private person. I like to spend the day at the beach, swimming. I bike to and from work. I read mysteries and have been known to go to South Beach clubs on occasion. I work more than anything."

"I can't imagine biking to work. That must be nice."

"Most days it is. The weather does get hot in midsummer, but I go in so early it doesn't much matter."

The waitress returned with their soup and salad. Their conversation turned to the books he had read. Many of them she had appreciated as well. They debated the pros and cons of the plots.

By the time they'd finished their meal, Melanie found she rather enjoyed Dalton's company. He had a way of drawing her out. Really listening to her opinions. She'd felt invisible for so long, it was nice being the center of someone's focus.

He paid for their dinner and they walked back to the mall door they'd entered.

"Time to bundle up." Melanie stopped beside a bench and began putting her coat on. Dalton placed his bag on the seat and helped her when she missed a sleeve with a hand. He then pulled his new jacket out of the large bag. It was a black wool pea jacket with a double row of buttons down the center. He slipped it on.

"Looks nice. But I would suggest that you not wear the tag." Melanie removed the paper hanging from under his arm. "You'll be much happier now."

"Wait—there's more." He dug into the sack again and pulled out a red and black scarf. Wrapping it around his neck, he flipped the ends over his shoulders and smiled broadly.

Melanie laughed. "Nice choice, but I don't think it'll keep you warm that way. Let me show you." She took the material and looped it around itself and pulled it up close to his neck, then she tucked the ends inside the lapel of his coat. Patting his chest with both hands, she met his gaze with a grin. "There."

Dalton wrapped his arms around her waist and pulled her close. "You deserve a proper thank-you for taking care of me," he whispered in a sandpapery voice as his mouth found hers.

His lips were warm and held a hint of whiskey. They were perfect. Her heart beat at record time. Her hands slid up to hold the ridge of his shoulders as Dalton pulled her tighter and the pressure of his mouth increased. Her body heated as if she were basking in the sun. His tongue traced the seam of her mouth. Her fingers seized his coat and she moaned. More, she wanted more. She returned his kiss.

Melanie had no idea how much time had passed before Dalton released her. Dazed, it took a few seconds before she realized that someone was clapping.

"I think we're making a scene," Dalton said as he picked up his bag and took her arm, leading her toward the door.

On unsteady legs, she went with him. *Wow! What a kiss.*

She glanced around to see a family grinning at them. "I guess we are." The words came out sounding shaky. The warmth of his lips still lingered on hers. A tingle lingered from his touch.

Dalton stopped on the sidewalk. "One more thing." He dug into the bag and came out with gloves.

"You thought of everything."

Pulling them on, he then stuffed the bag into the nearest trash can. He returned to her.

Not thinking about what she was doing, she ran her tongue along her bottom lip. His taste still remained.

Dalton groaned. "Please don't do that."

"What?"

He leaned in close. "Lick your lips. If you do it again I might really make a public scene."

Melanie felt hot despite the temperature being low

enough for snow to fall. Dalton had been as turned on as her. "We should get out of this cold."

"I'm ready when you are."

Something about his last statement made her think it might have a deeper meaning. One she wasn't sure she was prepared to deal with.

An hour later when Melanie pulled under the portico of the Lodge, Dalton still hadn't recovered from kissing her. He wanted her.

When she'd looked at him with that sparkle of mischief in her eyes and the smile that made her lovelier than any other woman he'd ever seen, he couldn't help himself. He had to taste her. She had no idea how desirable she was. Now, he wanted more than a kiss. If that one was any indication, the electricity between them would be powerful. Why couldn't they enjoy each other while he was here?

"How about coming up?"

"I don't know…"

"Come on. We could watch a movie." He wasn't interested in a movie but he would do whatever it took to spend some more time with Melanie.

"Do you feel up to having company? I would think you'd be tired and hurting."

He was hurting but it had nothing to do with being hit. "I am but I would be doing that anyway. The pain relievers have helped. So come on."

"Okay." She pulled on through the entryway and found a parking spot nearby.

At the door of his suite she hesitated. "Maybe—"

"Look, you didn't have a problem coming in when you insisted that you needed to be here for me. There shouldn't be any big deal to spending an evening watching TV with a friend."

She stopped short.

"Don't look so surprised. I think we've become friends

after today." That had been more than a friendly kiss. But he wasn't going to mention that and scare her away.

"I guess we have."

"What's the problem? Don't you think we can be friends?"

"No...yes. I don't know. I just don't spend a lot of time in men's hotel rooms."

"You could have fooled me. You were here all last night."

She pursed her lips. "You know what I mean. I think you're making fun of me now." She started down the hall toward the stairs.

He grabbed her arm, stopping her. "Maybe a little bit. Come on in. I can use the company. After all, I don't really know anyone else in town."

"Now you're playing on my sympathy." She hesitated another moment. "Okay, for just a little while."

Dalton let go of her arm and then unlocked the door. Melanie stepped into the suite. He joined her and closed the door. He walked to the coffee table and picked up the remote control to the large-screen TV and handed it to her. "Here, pick out something you'd like to watch while I put up my new clothes."

He came out of the bedroom a few minutes later, and found the TV off and Melanie sitting in one of the swivel chairs facing the window with the view of the falls. She didn't even react to his presence until he sat in the matching chair, and then only to glance at him. Neither of them said anything for a long time.

"I love the falls," she murmured. "They're so beautiful, but when the snow is on the ground and ice forms... it's magical."

"Have you always lived in Niagara Falls?"

"Heavens, no. I've lived in a number of places. You go where the football job is. Most coaches don't last but a few years if they aren't winning and only a few more if they are. Only when Dad became the general manager and I got the team physician position have I managed to stay in one place for a while."

"I hated moving around as a kid."

What had made him say that? He didn't talk about his childhood. That was a dark time in his life. Somehow Melanie made him feel safe to do so.

"I know what you mean. I don't know if I'll ever move away from here. Anyway, you can't get this just anywhere." She indicated the falls.

"You're right, but there are other wonderful places to live. Next to the beach, for example."

"It has been so long since I've been to the beach I can hardly remember what it's like."

"You're welcome to visit me anytime. My place is just across the road from the water. Take your towel and spend the day."

She looked at him for a second. "I'm sure I would interfere with your lifestyle."

"Is that your subtle way of asking if I'm dating someone?"

"Maybe. I'm not used to men inviting me to stay in their homes. I wouldn't want to step on some woman's toes."

Dalton glanced at her. He dated but never seriously. In fact, she was the first female he'd ever invited to spend any length of time in his home. With Melanie he was making a number of firsts. "I was just making a friendly offer. No pressure. You could always stay at a hotel if you wanted to."

"And I would bet you're counting on me not showing up."

"I'd have to admit I would be shocked if you did."

They sat in silence for a few minutes. Dalton found it rather interesting that he wasn't uncomfortable just sitting there. Had he ever spent time with a woman appreciating a view? He did dinner, movies, clubs and sex but never looking at something as simple as water falling. He'd never given much thought to connecting to a woman on a level as simple as enjoying her presence because he didn't want to. They met each other's mutual needs and he was gone. He always made that clear up front. Being around Melanie was doing something strange to him.

She stood. "Thanks for the offer of a movie but I'm tired and I think I'd better go. One of us slept on the sofa last night."

"That was your call, not mine. There's a big nice bed in both the rooms." The chair rocked softly as he stood.

"I guess I'm not going to make you feel guilty." Melanie moved toward the door.

"No, that's not going to happen. If you leave, who's going to make sure I can undress myself?"

"Now who's making who feel guilty? I think you'll manage."

"Is there no way I can talk you into staying?" Dalton moved closer, taking one of her hands.

"Dalton, I'm not sure what you're trying to talk me into here."

He reached an arm around her waist and pulled her close. His hand went behind her neck, bringing her face to his. "I've been thinking about nothing but kissing you again since we left the mall."

His lips found hers.

After a second her hands came to rest at his waist and started up his sides. He groaned.

She jerked away. "I'm sorry. I forgot."

"It doesn't matter." He brought her back to him. His lips found hers again. Melanie's hands went up his arms to grip his biceps. Her chest pressed against his as she leaned into him and returned his kisses. He teased her mouth and she opened for him. Their tongues mated and drove his desire for her higher.

Dalton pulled back and whispered, "Stay."

"Why?"

The question punched him in the gut. How did he answer that? *Because I want your body. Because it would be a way to pass the time.* What could he say that Melanie might accept?

She was no doubt looking for more than he was willing to take a chance on. He had only the truth. "Come on—it's not a big mystery. You're a healthy woman and I'm a healthy man. We're attracted to each other. Our kisses proved it. I thought we might have a good time together."

"So you've decided that since you're stuck here that I might be a little entertainment."

That statement didn't make him feel any better. Short-term was all he could offer. "That's not exactly accurate."

"Dalton, I'm flattered by the offer, I really am, but I'm not someone's one- or two-night stand. Let's not mess up what's becoming a nice friendship. I'll call you in the morning and see if you feel like you can fly. If so, I'll see about getting you a flight out."

Had he just been shot down? Dalton wasn't pleased with this twist of events. Melanie had turned the tables on him and taken the upper hand, made his suggestion sound like an insult. He had lost control of the situation. "Now wait a minute, Melanie, I think you've got this all wrong."

"No, I think I understood clearly. I'll call you in the morning."

She was gone before he could comprehend what had happened. If their kiss was any indication, she'd enjoyed it. But she was running from anything more. Maybe it was just as well. He wasn't looking for permanency and she'd all but told him he wouldn't do.

He'd learned long ago that having someone in his life to care and be around wasn't in the stars for him. They would only leave. He'd taken control of his life. Had built one that didn't depend on anyone but himself. Melanie didn't fit into the world he'd created for himself. Still, he enjoyed her far more than he'd liked any woman in a long time.

So why did it hurt so much when Melanie closed the door behind her?

CHAPTER FIVE

MELANIE RELIVED HER and Dalton's kiss over and over during the night. She'd been kissed before but never with the same breathtaking power, leaving her weak-kneed, heart pounding. Still she didn't know what he wanted from her.

She'd been mistaken about him when they'd first met. But she'd been wrong about another man and that mistake had taken her months to recover from. She couldn't trust her judgment, especially when Dalton's kiss had left her breathless. Her emotions had been played with once before and she refused to let that happen to her again.

When Dalton had arrived she'd questioned if he would be supportive of player care or succumb to pressure from the management to put Rocket back on the field. Thankfully, they were on the same side about what Rocket should do.

All the worrying and the angst didn't matter anyway because Dalton would be gone soon. They lived the length of the country from each other. Their paths weren't any more likely to cross than they had so far.

The wind howling made her question how bad the weather had become. Getting out of bed, she went to the kitchen and started the coffee machine before clicking on the TV. Pushing the button on the remote, she located the weather channel. A storm was affecting the entire east coast. Dalton wouldn't be pleased—he wouldn't be leaving today.

She called the Lodge and asked for his room. A few minutes later a drowsy-sounding Dalton struggled to say, "Hello?"

"I'm sorry but I have some bad news for you."

"Good morning to you too, Melanie." His voice sounded clearer. "You kept me up last night."

How could the man manage to get her heart pounding with a few simple words? It was nice to know that their kisses had disturbed him as well. She needed to get things back on a business level.

"Uh, I hate to tell you this but you're not going to get a flight out today. There's a major weather front coming in."

Melanie was surprised when there wasn't a large groan of disappointment on the other end of the line. She would miss him when he was gone.

"I figured that might be the case when I looked out the window this morning."

Imagining him still in bed with the covers tangled around his waist, his bare chest dark against the white sheets and the snow falling, had her wishing she wasn't talking to him over the phone but in person.

"So if I can't go home today, what're we going to do?"

The vision of him in bed popped into her mind again. She needed to stop thinking of him that way. They wanted two different things. "Well, I'm going to practice in a few hours. I have a couple of the players to check in with and preparations to make for the game tomorrow. Also I need to double-check Rocket."

"I think I'll go along. Better than being stuck here."

With a note of humor in her voice she said, "I missed the part where you were invited."

"Come on, Melanie, you know you enjoy having me around."

She huffed. Admitting he was right wasn't something

she was prepared to do. Even after spending three full days with him, she found she'd missed him last night. "How're you feeling, by the way?"

"Stiff, but I'll live. A hot shower will help with that. Want to come over? I might need help drying off."

Now she was really having a hard time concentrating on what she had to say. "If you're going with me, be ready in an hour."

His soft chuckle filled her ear before she disconnected the call.

Dalton liked watching Melanie work. She had a real rapport with the players and staff. There was a firm but gentle manner to her care. A couple of times she'd even asked him if he was willing to give his opinion. He'd gladly done so.

It shocked him that he wasn't more upset about not being able to get a flight home. In fact, when Melanie had picked him up she'd told him he might not get out until after Christmas. He wasn't pleased but what could he do? With the snow and the holiday plane traffic, he'd be here at least another four days. More time to get to know Melanie. He'd flown in with every intention of leaving within twenty-four hours and here he was, almost glad he was stuck in Niagara Falls.

One of the players came in. "Hey, Doc, can you give my neck a look?"

"Sure, Crush, have a seat." Melanie directed the huge man to a stool.

Dalton assumed she'd asked him to sit there because she wouldn't be able to reach his neck otherwise. Melanie wasn't a tiny woman but around all the extralarge men she was dwarfed in comparison. Still she had an air of authority.

Fifteen minutes later Crush had been put under the care of a trainer for a heat compression to his neck.

"What's the deal with everyone having a nickname?"

Dalton asked. "Is that the thing to have if you play foot-ball? There's Rocket and Crush and you are even called Mel instead of Melanie. Doesn't anyone go by their real name?"

She shrugged. "I don't know. In some cases it's some-one's ability, in others a sign of affection and others it could be something embarrassing they have done in the past and now it's just part of them. Why? You don't like nicknames?"

He knew what it was like to have a past filled with neg-ative names. "No, I don't."

Melanie stopped what she was doing and looked at him. "Why not?"

"I guess I was called an ugly one too many times as a kid." There he was, doing it again. He'd never told anyone that. Saying it somehow made it not feel so heavy anymore.

"I'm sorry."

"Nothing for you to be sorry about. It was a long time ago. I've gotten over it."

Melanie looked at him for a moment. Did she believe him?

A few more players came in with complaints. She checked them out and sent them to the trainers to use the exercise bikes to warm up.

At one point Rocket entered the room. "Hey, Doc Mel. Hello, Dr. Reynolds."

"You here to have your knee wrapped?" Melanie asked.

"Yeah. Not having any problems but I'm doing as you say."

"You can't be too careful," Dalton said. "Take care of it. You don't want it to get worse. I'm still unsure about you playing tomorrow."

"I've got this, Doc. I'll be fine. The team needs me."

"Tomorrow, before the game, I want you at the stadium early in the morning," Melanie said.

"Will do," Rocket said over his shoulder as he pushed through the training room doors.

Melanie looked at the wall clock. "I'm headed out to the practice field. I'll understand if you'd rather stay here."

"Are you implying I might be scared?" Dalton had long overcome being intimidated by people playing games.

"Well..." she said with a grin.

He stood. "I can handle it."

Melanie gave him a sharp look. "Okay. Come on."

They walked the same pathway as they had two days earlier and entered the practice area. Again Melanie went to the midfield line and stopped. A number of players spoke to her as they jogged onto the field.

"Hey, man, I'm sorry."

Dalton looked at the gigantic man standing beside him. "What?"

"I'm the one who blindsided you and Doc Mel the other day. Man, I'm sorry. I was looking for the ball. Are you okay?"

"I'm fine. Doc Mel is also."

The man studied Melanie. "You sure?"

She placed her hand on the player's arm. "We're both fine, Juice."

The man's concern showed in the seriousness of his eyes. "Good. I sure was worried. I'm sorry that happened."

"It was an accident. I know that." Mel smiled at him.

Juice gave Dalton a questioning look.

Dalton offered the player his hand. "No hard feelings, I promise."

Obvious relief covered his face. "Thanks, man, I really appreciate that."

"Juice, let's go," Coach Rizzo called from the center of the field.

Dalton watched as the player loped out onto the field.

"Thanks for being so understanding. Juice is one of

those tender-hearted guys I was talking about. I'm sure he lost sleep over what happened."

Dalton faced her. "Hey, I understand when accidents happen. I'm not such an ogre I can't accept that."

"I wasn't so sure about that a few days ago," Melanie murmured.

"How's that?"

"You acted pretty uptight when you first arrived."

Had he come over that way? Despite being in control of his world, owning his own practice and being a sought-after surgeon, any time the idea of a game being more important than a person came up it put him on edge. He just didn't place the same value on winning that others did. "I was that bad?"

"You were pretty inflexible."

"You still think that about me?"

Melanie smiled. "I'm learning to appreciate other aspects of your personality."

Why did he all of a sudden want to thump his chest?

For over an hour they watched the players move around on the field without any close calls.

Finally Melanie said, "I've some paperwork to take care of. So I'm going to my office for a while."

"Since I'm staying here for a few more days I need to make some calls, change around my schedule. Is there a place where I can use a computer and talk in private?"

"There's an office next to the Performance Area that isn't in use. You're welcome to it."

"Great."

He made his calls. One to an associate at his practice, telling him to request Josey's records. If they showed what he thought they would, he believed he could help the girl.

An hour later Melanie knocked on the door of the office Dalton was using. "I have to do some shopping for my family's Christmas dinner. With the game tomorrow and Christmas Eve a few days after that, I won't have another chance. Do you want me to drop you off at the Lodge or arrange for you to get a ride back?"

Dalton couldn't remember the last time he'd been to a grocery store. Most of his meals were eaten in the hospital cafeteria or at a restaurant. Something about going to one with Melanie made it sound intriguing. It certainly sounded better than sitting in his room watching movies. "Mind if I come with you?"

Her look of shock was almost comical. "You want to go to the grocery store with me?"

"Don't act so surprised. I eat too."

She put her hands on her hips and glared at him. "When was the last time *you* went to the grocery store?"

"Okay, maybe I don't go often but it would be better than sitting in my room by myself."

"So I'm a step better than boredom."

He held her gaze. "I find you far from boring."

The air suddenly held an electric charge. "Um, you can go if you like but fair warning—it'll be a madhouse so don't expect it to be fun."

"I think I can handle it."

Melanie had to admit that Dalton was good help with grocery buying. He'd insisted on pushing the cart while she gathered the supplies she needed. It was a rather odd feeling to be spending an afternoon hour in the grocery with a man. It wasn't something she'd ever done before.

"You cook dinner for your entire family every Christmas Eve?"

"My sisters-in-law help. I do the majority of the meal but they bring the sides and desserts."

"Sounds like work."

"Not really. I enjoy it. Especially when I'm not pressed for time. This year, with the Currents in the playoffs, it will be more difficult. But I'm tickled to have the Currents doing so well. What do you usually do for a Christmas meal?"

"I go to a restaurant close to my condo for a meal with a few friends and then we spend the afternoon on the beach or beside a pool. Sometimes I'll have friends in for a catered meal but mostly it's a quiet day."

She looked at him as she placed four cans of beans in the cart. "You don't get together with family? What about your parents? Brothers and sisters?"

He was starting to think coming here with her might not have been such a good idea. "No parents. No siblings."

"I'm sorry."

"No need to be sorry. It's just the way it is."

That sounded rather sad to her. "It isn't quiet at the Hyde house. With seven kids running around, the TV on full volume, and my brothers and father armchair coaching. It is loud."

At least she wasn't asking him any more about his family.

"If you don't get to leave before Christmas you are welcome to join my family."

"I'll think about it."

Melanie moved around the turkeys, looking for the perfect one. Having picked one out, she lifted it toward the cart.

"Let me have that." Dalton took the turkey from her and placed it with the other food.

Melanie continued around the store until she had everything on her list. They loaded the groceries into the car. She offered to take Dalton back to the Lodge, but he insisted that he should help unload the groceries. She agreed. Melanie wasn't sure she was comfortable having him in her small condo. Could she resist him if he kissed her again?

By the time they had unloaded the bags at her condo, they were both cold.

"I don't see how you stand living in this winter." Dalton joined her at her door for the second time with bags of food. "I know why we have so many snowbirds now."

"I have to admit this is rather extreme." Melanie pushed the door open and went down the short hallway to the kitchen.

After Dalton had dumped his bags on the counter he stood looking at the space beyond, which was her living area.

What did those perceptive eyes see? "Is something wrong?"

"No, I was just thinking how much this place looks like you. I like it."

Her sitting room was filled with overstuffed furniture so that it was warm and comfortable. Bright pillows in red, green and yellow were situated on the couch and chairs. Books lined one wall. A couple of floor lamps sat so they hung over one end of the couch and a chair. Modern art pictures of flowers hung on the walls. A small tree with multicolored bulbs sat in a corner. Surrounding it on the floor were presents of all shapes and sizes.

"Thank you. I spend a lot of time here so I want it to be as inviting as possible." Stepping over to the tree, she plugged the lights in. She stood looking at them for a few seconds before she walked to the kitchen. There she started taking food items out of bags. "Why don't you sit down and I'll get us something warm to drink."

"Why don't you tell me where to find the coffee—?"

"I was thinking hot chocolate."

"Okay, hot chocolate. Then we both can sit down and rest for a minute."

"If I do that I might not get up again."

"I'll see that you do. So where's a pot and that hot chocolate?"

Melanie pulled packets of hot chocolate out of the

cabinet behind her. "The teapot is in the cabinet beside the oven. You can heat water in it."

Dalton found it and had water heating with the same efficiency he did everything else. While he did that, she stored away most of the food. They were still waiting on the water to get hot when she pulled out an onion and began chopping it for the dressing.

"Hey, what're you doing?"

"I can't waste time. I need to get busy with cooking this food."

"I think you can take five minutes for yourself. Go sit down. I think I can handle the hot chocolate."

She had to admit that it would be nice to sit, drink a cup of hot chocolate and close her eyes. "Okay, since you put it that way."

Melanie went to the couch, curled up in the corner, pulled her feet up and laid her head back. Her eyelids started to droop. She'd just close them for a minute.

She woke to warmth. There was a blanket covering her. The sun had set. A single lamp shone across the room. Dalton sat on the other end of the sofa reading a book. "Why did you let me go to sleep?"

He looked at her and closed the book. "Hey, I don't control that."

She threw the blanket back. "I've got to get busy."

"What's the hurry?"

"I've got food to prepare."

"What happens if you don't?" he said in a tone that implied she was overreacting.

"Then we won't have enough for the Christmas meal." She stood.

"And this would be the end of the world?"

Now he was starting to make her mad. "My family expects me to fix the turkey and dressing."

"And you wouldn't want to disappoint them." He made it sound as if her family was taking advantage of her. He put his book down. "To keep you from going into a panic, I'll help. Just assign me something easy."

"You don't have to."

"If it will stop you from feeling guilty over a nap, then I can help out."

"How about cutting onions?" she asked, heading for the kitchen.

"Why?"

"For the dressing. I wish you had woken me."

He joined her. "You needed to sleep. Between your job with the team, working at the hospital and taking care of me, you haven't had much downtime in the last few days. I kind of liked listening to you snore."

"Hey, I don't snore!" She gave him a light swat on the forearm.

"I think the lady doth protest too much, especially when she does."

They both laughed. She'd not had this much fun in a long time. She would miss Dalton when he was gone. Too much, she was afraid. "You're so bad."

"Thank you."

"That wasn't meant as a compliment." She turned and pulled a cookbook off a shelf. "The onions are in a bag under that cabinet." Melanie pointed just past him. "Here is the knife and cutting board." She pulled them out of a drawer.

Dalton took the items from her. "I hope you don't expect my chopping to be perfect."

She met his gaze. At least he'd offered to help—something that her father or brothers wouldn't think to do. "I can't imagine you not being confident about your ability in anything."

Dalton's eyes darkened for a second, then cleared. Had she said something wrong? "I'm going to start making the cornbread." She pulled the cornmeal out from under the cabinet.

A few minutes later he ran a finger down her cheek when she came to check on his progress.

"Please don't."

Why had his simple touch made her want to lean into his heat and not leave?

"Are you scared of what I might do or is it because you're afraid of what you might do?"

If she was truthful, it was both, but she couldn't say that. "I thought we were going to keep things between us friendly."

"I was just getting your attention to ask if you had given any thought to dinner."

"No."

"Then it's a good thing that I have. I found a magnet stuck to your refrigerator with a pizza place on it while you were snoring. I ordered cheese and pepperoni. Should be here soon. I hope that's okay with you."

Melanie stepped back before she did something she might regret. Like hugging him. "Sounds perfect." Surprisingly, she was finding more and more things about Dalton that were perfect.

An hour later Dalton pushed his chair back from Melanie's café-style table and said, "It's been a long time since I've had a pizza that good."

"It's my favorite. I lived off pizza when I was a kid. The only thing my father knew to do for meals was cook frozen pizza or order in."

"It isn't easy to lose a mother when you're young."

"No. You sound like you understand."

He wasn't sure he wanted to discuss his mother in general and certainly not in particular. "I have a pretty good idea."

"You said your parents were gone. How old were you when they died?"

She wouldn't let it go. Would it really hurt him to tell

his story? "Only my mother has died, as far as I know. I have no idea about my father."

"But you said—"

"They are dead to me. My father went to prison when I was a couple of months old. I never really knew him. I was taken from my mother when I was six. She died a couple of years later in jail." It wasn't as painful to tell Melanie as he'd thought it might be. Something about her made him believe she wouldn't judge.

"I'm sorry. We have more in common than I thought. We both lost our mothers."

This was getting far too personal for his taste. She made it sound as if they had a bond that would always bind them in a special way.

"So where did you live?"

"Foster homes. More than one, actually."

"That couldn't have been easy. At least I had my father and brothers. Even though they weren't around much. Mostly it was just Coach and me."

He liked that she had turned the focus off of him. "Your father wasn't around much either, was he?"

"No. But I always knew he cared about me."

"That was a good thing." He had been thirteen or fourteen before he'd thought someone actually cared about him. Mrs. Richie had been that person but she'd soon pushed him away as well. Trusting a person to have his back was something he had a difficult time doing.

She nodded. "It was. There were times I wished he understood me better. But my dad was more about guys than girls. I don't even know why I'm telling you this."

Dalton knew what it was like not to be understood. He took another swallow of his drink. "What're friends for?"

"It's not to dump the past on. I do know that." She rose and started cleaning the table. "I hate to put a man out in the cold but I need to take you to the Lodge. I have to be up early to get ready for the game."

"Do you mind me going with you? Since I'm here I might as well check on Rocket if he plays."

"No, I'd be glad to have you on the sideline but I want to warn you it'll be freezing. There's supposed to be some sun but only in the late afternoon."

"Great. I'll be looking forward to it." There wasn't much enthusiasm in his words.

"You don't sound like it. I'll stop by Coach's house early and get a few of my brother's old gloves and a hat for you. See if I can find some boots."

"Maybe that way I won't freeze."

"There are warmers you can stand beside so that doesn't happen."

When was the last time he'd not been prepared for what life brought him? Long ago he'd learned the importance of being ready. If you were prepared, then you were in control of what happened. Nothing about this trip, outside of caring for Rocket, had gone as he had planned. To his astonishment, it didn't seem to upset him as much as it should have. He was learning to appreciate the wonder of what might transpire.

His friends in Miami would hoot when he told them he'd gone to a pro football game. And probably fall on the floor laughing when they found out he'd stood in the snow on the sideline. Dalton smiled to himself. He should give some thought to whether or not to tell them about this trip. The teasing might be more than he could take.

"Come on, I'll take you to the Lodge," Melanie said as she picked up her coat off the chair where she'd left it earlier.

"Gee, I thought I might get an invite to stay the night." His tone was flippant but he wouldn't hesitate to take her up on the offer if she made it.

"Dalton—" Her voice sounded unsure.

"I'm just kidding. I wasn't planning to spend the night." Her apparent relief pricked his feelings. "I'll call a taxi.

No need for you to go out." He pulled out his cell phone and searched for a car service.

"I don't mind taking you."

"It's not a problem." He dialed the number of the service and spoke to them. After disconnecting he said, "They should be here in about fifteen minutes."

"Okay." Melanie sounded sad. She dropped her coat on the chair again and stepped toward him.

His look locked with hers.

"I'm sorry, Dalton. I'm not a very good flirt. Not like the saleswoman. I've seen too many women make fools of themselves over players. Even my own brothers. I'm not that kind of person. I don't invite men to stay. I'm not a short wow person. I'm more of the cautious, get-to-know-you-slowly type."

Dalton came closer and cupped her face. His thumb caressed the curve of her cheek. "Short wow, huh? I've not heard that before. I really was teasing about staying. There's nothing for you to feel bad about. If it isn't for you, it isn't for you."

A few minutes of uncomfortable silence filled the space between them. Why had he asked about staying? He wanted that easy interaction between them back. His phone buzzed and he answered it. "I'll be right out." To her, he said, "Taxi's here." Turning away from Melanie, he pulled his coat on, wrapped his scarf around his neck the way she'd shown him. "What time will you pick me up in the morning?"

"Eight."

"I'll be waiting in the lobby. Don't come in. I'll watch for you." He went to the door.

"Dalton…"

He turned to find Melanie right behind him. She grabbed the lapels of his coat, stood on her toes and brought her mouth to his. Her lips were damp, as if she'd just run her tongue across them with indecision. They quivered slightly. The kiss was sweet, sensuous and sincere. And entirely too short.

"See you tomorrow." She sounded a little breathless.

Wow. He had a feeling he was headed in a direction he hadn't planned to go and wasn't sure he could control.

CHAPTER SIX

MELANIE PULLED HER car into the slot designated as hers at the stadium. The other spots were slowly filling up as the players and staff arrived.

Dalton had been waiting in the lobby, just as he'd said he would. Her face turned warm as she watched him walk toward the car. That was all it took for her body to hum. It was becoming more difficult for her to keep her distance. Being impulsive was so unlike her. She still couldn't believe she'd kissed him after she'd told him they should only be friends. Had she opened the door to rejection again? Thank goodness he seemed at ease as they drove to the stadium. She was relieved he didn't mention the kiss.

Pulling a bag along with her medical one out of the backseat, she joined Dalton at the front of the car. She handed the bigger one to him. "Your warm clothes."

"Thanks." He glanced at the sky, where gray clouds gathered. "I'm going to need them."

She nodded.

"What's going on with you? It's like there is a hum of electricity about you."

"I guess it's excitement." Great—he'd noticed. This was a healthy direction. She led him through a large roll-up door opening big enough for a transfer truck to completely enter.

"What are we in, a wind tunnel?"

Melanie pushed her hair out of her face. "It's like this all the time. Even in the summer. It's caused by the air coming off the field though the tunnels."

They took a ramp and entered another door into a warm, long hallway. Melanie walked ahead of Dalton but she was aware of him close behind her. Too aware.

Never a forward person where men were concerned and still not sure she wasn't making the wrong step, Melanie was still glad she'd kissed him. When she'd told him he wasn't invited to stay she hadn't missed that dark look of rejection in his eyes. Something about his expression made her think it was a deep-seated emotion that Dalton felt more than the average person. She didn't want him to leave her place thinking she wasn't attracted to him. Who was she kidding? She wanted him on a level she'd never felt before but she had no doubt he would break her heart. They didn't want the same things in a relationship.

Today she had a job to do and thinking about Dalton wasn't the best way to do a quality one. Treating him like the visiting professional was what she needed to do.

At another door, she turned the knob and opened it. "This is the Currents' locker room."

This was her space. Next door was the training room and beyond that the dressing room. She placed her bag on the desk. "You can leave that—" she indicated the bag Dalton carried "—on that chair. Most of my time will be spent next door until the game starts. Then I'll be on the sideline. I'd be glad to have someone take you up to the Manager's box if you'd like."

"No, I'd rather see what you do."

Melanie liked the idea of Dalton being interested in her part of the medical profession. She'd had the impression when they'd first met that he didn't think too highly of it. Maybe today he'd completely change his opinion.

"Well, just know the option is always there. It's warm and there's food."

"Please don't tempt me." He grinned.

"It's time for me to check in with the trainers. They'll already be taping some ankles and caring for knees of the players that arrived early."

"I'd be interested to see how that's being done. I'm only involved in the surgery when a repair is needed, never on the preemptive side. It would be beneficial to watch it done."

"Help yourself. You can see plenty of it today."

Dalton left her for the training room. A couple of times when a player pushed through the doors to her office Dalton's voice carried as he questioned someone about why they were doing it that way. Once his laugh mixed with one of the player's.

It fascinated her that he seemed to interact with the players so well when he had no interest in the game. Or at least that was what he'd claimed. She hadn't thought he'd be comfortable with the players. Now he seemed interested in at least getting to know the team on a medical level.

Soon it was time for the team to go out on the field for the pregame warm-up. She joined Dalton in the training room.

"While they're out doing warm-ups I'm going up to say hello to Marcus. Would you like to come?"

"Sure. Do I need to put on my warmer layer?"

"That's not necessary. We'll be in the building the entire time." She went out the door and Dalton followed her. When he'd arrived less than a week ago she would have never believed she'd still be entertaining him. It was funny how life took twists and turns. Dalton might be hanging out with her because he had nothing better to do, but she was enjoying having him around. Especially when he kissed her. Melanie glanced at him. That was something she was better off not thinking about.

They took an elevator that dropped them off in a concourse carpeted in black and yellow—the Currents' colors.

A security guard stood just outside the elevator. "Why, hello, Doc. I haven't seen you in some time. It's good to see you."

"Hi, Benny. Nice to see you too. How's that new grand-baby doing?"

"Growing like a weed. Growing like a weed."

"That's great."

As they walked away Dalton asked, "Do you know everyone?"

"Don't you know the people where you work?" Surely he was on friendly terms with the people in the hospital where he did surgery. This was her place of work, just like that was his.

They walked on until they came to the Currents' staff family box that was on the forty-five-yard line.

Melanie pushed the door open and Dalton followed.

The back of Marcus's dark head was all she could see. She smiled. He had his nose pressed against the glass. A fog ring had formed in front of his mouth.

Snow fell outside to the point that in order to see the lines on the field, the snow had to be blown away.

"How's the front-row seat, Marcus?" At her question, the boy turned around.

There was a large smile on his face. "This is awesome. Thanks, Dr. Mel."

She took the chair next to him while Dalton stood nearby. On the other side of Marcus sat an older woman with gray in her tight curls. Melanie smiled at her.

"This is my grandmother," Marcus offered. "She's a big Currents fan."

The woman smiled at Melanie. "I'm Lucinda Aberna-thy. Thanks for doing this for Marcus. He'll remember it forever."

"You're welcome. I'm glad I could. Marcus, look who came with me?" She glanced back at Dalton.

Marcus smiled. "Hi, Doc."

"Hey, Marcus. How're you feeling?"

"Much better since I've been let out of the hospital for a while."

"I can understand that. It's been rather nice for me not to be in one all the time too."

Melanie looked at him. That was an interesting statement. He couldn't get back to Miami fast enough the other day and surgeons were known for spending large amounts of time in an OR.

She spoke to Marcus and his grandmother. "Have either of you tried the buffet?"

"Is that for us too?" Marcus asked as if he thought it might be too good to be true.

"Sure it is. Do you mind if Dr. Reynolds and I eat lunch with you and your grandmother?"

"No."

"Then let's eat." Melanie moved so that Marcus and his grandmother could come by her and be first in line. She said to Dalton, "This is our chance for a meal. We don't get another until well after the game."

"I'm hungry so this is a great time." He leaned in closer as if he didn't want anyone else to hear. "Without you spending the night and telling me what to do, I didn't get up in time to have breakfast."

"Shh," Melanie hissed as she walked to where the food was being served. Dalton was teasing her but still it made her blood flow warm just to think about *what if*.

He stood close behind her. His breath ruffled her hair when he whispered, "I'm really hungry."

Melanie poked her elbow in his ribs.

"Aww," he grunted.

She whirled around. "I'm so sorry. I forgot." She took his arm that wasn't holding his side. "Sit down. Sit down."

He settled into a nearby chair. "I'm fine. Really."

"I hurt you." She went down on a knee so she could see his face.

"I got what I deserved for picking at you."

"Are you hurt, Doc?" Marcus asked as he and his grand-mother stood staring at them with full plates in their hands.

"I'm fine. Juice used me as... What are those things called that football players hit?"

"A blocking dummy," Marcus said with complete confidence. "You got hit by Juice? How cool."

"It wasn't so cool at the time." Dalton groaned as he turned in his chair. "Not so cool at this minute either."

Melanie's heart tightened. She'd have to put Dalton on the plane soon before she managed to beat him to death. "I'll get you a plate."

"I'm not going to argue."

Melanie was afraid she might cry. Dalton took her fingers in his and gave them a squeeze. "I'm going to live. Just give me a minute to catch my breath."

"Okay."

"Now, I'm going to move over to the table with Marcus and his grandmother. We'll save you a seat."

She gave him a weak smile. "Do you like your burger all the way?"

"Everything but onions. I might get up close and personal with someone before the day is out."

Melanie was glad that their lunch partners had found the table set up in the back of the room. "Do you need help getting there?"

"Melanie, I feel emasculated enough without you making me an invalid."

She bit her lip. Was she making it that bad? "All right. I'll try to show you as little concern as possible."

"Hey, don't go overboard. I like your attention."

She gave him a wry grin. "I think that's what got you into this situation."

Dalton had the good grace to give a wry smile. "That it did."

"I'll get your burger. You get yourself to the table." Melanie turned her back to him. It was tough to resist helping him, but maybe he was right, she was fussing too much.

Dalton remained at the table with Marcus when his grand-mother and Melanie went to pick out desserts. "So you didn't have any guys begging you to bring them to the game?"

Marcus shrugged. "Sure, but I rather they come be-cause they are my friend not just because I had cool seats for the game."

"So you think your friends might be using you?"

"When you're a sick kid you learn real quick who your friends are. I have a couple of good ones and couldn't bring them both. My grandmother watches every Currents game. I had to bring her or she would have killed me."

Dalton chuckled. "I guess you didn't have a choice."

"Naw."

"So when you grow up, what do you want to be?"

"I'd like to be a history teacher."

Dalton nodded. He hadn't expected that as an answer. "That sounds like a good plan."

"I like to read about history and go to forts and muse-ums. Some of my friends make fun of me, but my grand-mother says not to pay them any attention."

"Some guys just don't get it. You grandmother's right. I'm glad you have her. You'll end up being the smart guy who teaches those guys' children."

Dalton knew well the importance of having someone to cheer you on. He hadn't had anyone. Yet something deep inside him still wanted to make Mrs. Richie proud. "Keep up your studies and make your grandmother happy."

"I will."

Melanie and Marcus's grandmother returned. Placing a plate with three different desserts in front of him, Mel-anie then sat in the chair next to his. "I've got to go in a few minutes. If you'd like to stay here and watch the game with Marcus you're welcome to."

"Are you trying to get rid of me?"

"No, but you may wish you had by halftime."

"If I'm going to really keep an eye on Rocket, then I need to be on the field."

"That's true."

They made their way back to the Currents' locker room area. This time Dalton didn't follow. He walked confidently beside Melanie. When they arrived at the office again, Melanie said, "I keep the clothes I need in a locker in the bathroom. I'll lock the doors and you can dress in here. I found some of my brother's old long underwear. I think you'll be glad I did. Be ready to go in a few minutes."

Her tone implied that if he wasn't he'd be left behind.

He was tall enough that the snow suit she'd brought him fit well when it was zipped up the front. The boots were large but not so much so they were clown size and difficult to walk in. They were well lined and he was positive he would be glad to have them on.

Melanie came out of the bathroom dressed much as he was. "We need to get moving. It's time for the team to go to the field."

The wind pushed them backward as they made their way out of the tunnel behind the team. They ran onto the field while he and Melanie walked to the sideline.

"Feel free to stand by the warmers but don't get too close because they can melt your overalls."

By the middle of the second quarter of the game, Dalton was stomping his feet and standing beside a warmer. Snow blew as the wind picked up, producing mini tornados around his feet. Still the stands were filled with people shouting as the players moved the ball first one way and then another. He didn't understand all the penalties or the nuances of the game but he had to admit it was easy to get caught up in the excitement. He marched up and down the sideline beside Melanie as the team changed ends. She was completely into the game. Occasionally, she would holler and jump up and down. What would it take to have her that enthusiastic about him?

Rocket played well and there was no indication that his knee was giving him any problems. After a play, one of the men didn't immediately get up. Melanie and a couple of the trainers wearing medical packs around their waists ran out on the field. Soon the player was being helped to the side as Melanie gave him her complete attention.

At halftime they went into the locker room with the players. He was thankful for the warmth. The only problem was that it didn't last long enough. They had to return to the field about the time feeling returned to his toes. He hated this weather.

Melanie grinned as they made their way up the tunnel. "You sure you wouldn't rather be in the heated, glassed-in box with Marcus?"

He groaned. "Please don't tempt me." Dalton kept walking. He was determined to impress her by sticking out the game.

It was the middle of the third quarter and the Currents were winning when another player was injured. Melanie jogged onto the field once again. A group of players and staff surrounded the man lying on the ground.

For a few seconds there was complete silence in the stadium. Melanie stepped outside of the circle and waved him toward her. She didn't wait on him to arrive; instead, she returned to the center of the circle. Hurrying as fast as he could without slipping on the icy ground, Dalton made his way halfway across the field. It was much farther than it looked. As he reached the group, they opened for him.

Melanie was on her knees beside the groaning player. She saw Dalton and moved so that he could kneel beside her at the player's thigh. His cleat had been removed. A plastic sheet was beneath him. A blanket had also been thrown across the man's shoulders.

"What do you think? Broken or fractured Lisfranc joint?" Melanie asked, looking at Dalton.

"Hey, Doc," the player called, "it hurts but I can play."

Dalton and Melanie ignored the statement. He placed the palm of his hand over the top of the foot and found it was already swelling. Moving over and around Melanie, Dalton went to the feet of the player. "We need to cut the sock off."

Melanie was handed scissors by one of the trainers. With efficacy of movement she had the sock removed. While she was busy doing that, he took off his gloves. Before he touched the player Dalton rubbed his hands together to make them as warm as possible. Placing his fingers on either side of the foot, he worked his way over the bones. As he touched the top of it the man winced.

Melanie was right. "I think it's a fracture, but we need an X-ray to confirm."

"Call for the cart," she said loudly and a couple of the staff broke away from the group to do her bidding.

Dalton stood and Melanie did too as the cart arrived. She oversaw the player being loaded. When he was ready to be taken off the field, she said to Dalton, "I'm going with Mitchell to the locker room to see that he's taken care of until the ambulance arrives."

"I'll come along." Dalton started to add *if you need help*, but she wouldn't. Melanie had handled the situation with professionalism and quality of care. He'd been impressed. There was more to being a team doctor than he'd believed.

She'd seen to it that the ankle as well as the leg had been immobilized when they reached the medical area. Few he'd seen could have done it better. While she worked, the TV mounted high on the wall blared the game.

There had been another couple of touchdowns and the faint roar of the crowd reached them under the stands.

Everyone, except him, reacted outwardly to each of them. He had to admit there had been a wish to throw his hands up as the Currents crossed over the line and a tug of disappointment when the other team took the lead again. By the time the ambulance arrived, there were only a few minutes left in the game and the Currents had the ball.

"Come on, Doc," Mitchell said to Melanie as she gave her report to the EMT, "let me stay until the game is over." He'd been give pain medicine and was feeling better.

"We have it on in the wagon," he heard one of the EMTs assure Mitchell.

The player was being whisked out the large roll-up door Melanie and he had walked through that morning. The TV was still on and a couple of the staff had stopped what they were doing to stand looking up at it. Melanie joined them and he stood beside her.

The Currents were on the two-yard line. If they made this play they would win the game. A thud from the pounding of feet came from above. It seemed as if everyone in the room held their breath.

The quarterback handed off the ball to number twenty-one, who Dalton had learned was Rocket. He made a move to the left, not being caught by the two men chasing him, then he cut to the right to dodge another man. He jumped a pile of men tangled up on the goal line and fell into the end zone. The crowd erupted into a roar as the last second ticked off the clock. The Currents had won the game.

"We won. We won." Melanie jumped up and down and then threw her arms around Dalton's neck and kissed him.

His arms circled her waist and he passionately returned her kiss.

Melanie broke away. "I'm sorry. I got carried away."

"I'm not." But next time he wanted her to kiss him because of him.

They looked at the TV again. His team members were slapping Rocket on the back. When they finally climbed off him and let him stand, Rocket struggled to do so.

In unison Dalton and Melanie said, "His knee."

CHAPTER SEVEN

MELANIE SHOVED THROUGH the doors and started running up the tunnel toward the arena. Dalton was right behind her. As they approached the field, people started coming in the other direction. Soon they were fighting against the tide. Dalton went past her and created a path for her to follow. It was nice to have him looking after her.

They finally made their way to the bench on the sideline where Rocket was sitting. A number of players, staff, Coach Rizzo, her father and some of the media stood close by. A couple of the heaters had been moved to either side of him and his winter game cape had been placed over his shoulders.

"Rocket, we saw it on TV. How's your knee feeling?" Melanie asked in a panting voice.

"Hey, Doc. Doc Reynolds. I thought you might be showing up."

"So how is it?" Dalton was already down on a knee in front of Rocket.

Melanie had forgotten to put on her outer clothes. Dalton wasn't wearing his coat, hat or gloves either. He must be cold. She sure was. But Dalton didn't show it. His concern was focused on Rocket.

"I'm going to have to put my hands on you. I'm afraid they aren't warm," Dalton told Rocket.

"Don't worry. I'm so cold that I probably can't feel you anyway."

"I'll make it quick. Then we'll *all* go inside."

Dalton did the same type of exam he'd done at their first meeting. Except his face grew more thoughtful this time.

Finished, he stood. "I don't want you walking on this leg. You need to have an X-ray and MRI ASAP."

"Let's get the cart back out here," Melanie told one of the staff.

"I really did it this time," Rocket said.

"I'm afraid today might be it for you this year." Dalton put his hands under his armpits and stomped the ground. One of the trainers put a blanket over his shoulders and also handed her one.

"We need him for next week," Coach Rizzo protested. "Even bigger game than this."

Her father glanced at the media, busy flashing pictures. "We don't need to make that decision until after the tests are done. This is something better discussed when we have all the information."

Dalton looked at her as if expecting her to disagree with her father.

"That sounds like a wise plan. We won't know anything for a couple of days," Melanie offered in a conciliatory tone.

Dalton gave her a disappointed look, then headed for the tunnel leading to the locker room.

The cart pulled up close to Rocket and Melanie stayed with him until he was being driven off the field. While the trainer prepared Rocket for his trip to the emergency room, she went to her office to change.

Dalton was sitting in a chair with one ankle over a knee, his outer clothes already removed. His look met hers when she entered.

"I'm freezing. That's the last time I'm running out without at least my overcoat." She pulled the blanket closer around her.

"I'm almost warm. But my toes are still burning," Dalton said flatly.

"We'll be out of here soon. I have to go to the hospital to check on Mitchell and see that Rocket gets those tests run. I'm assuming you want to go with me."

"Will you be taking any of my advice if I do?"

She stopped halfway into the bathroom. "What does that mean?"

"It means you know that Rocket shouldn't play in any more games until that knee heals. Why didn't you say so?"

"Because we don't know that for sure until after we do the tests and because you never make those type of statements in front of the media. The Currents are in the playoffs for the first time in franchise history. Rocket is an important part of making that happen. If the other team thinks Rocket won't be there, it might not give them a physical advantage but it will certainly give them a mental one. The same goes for our team. We can't have them believing Rocket is out before it's a fact. It affects them mentally as well."

"You have to be kidding. One player carries that much weight?"

"I'm not and he does." She continued on into the bathroom. Why couldn't he believe that winning the game was important?

Melanie stepped out again and looked at him. "Didn't you see how the fans reacted today? Hear Marcus talking about his grandmother's love for the Currents?"

"But is a win worth the price of a man being crippled for the rest of his life?"

What kind of a person did he think she was? "No, it isn't. I don't think so as a person and I certainly don't believe that as a doctor. All I'm saying is that we need to take it slow, know what we're talking about."

Dalton seemed to consider that. He uncrossed his leg and put his hands on his knees. "I can agree with that. As long as I know whose side you're on."

"Side? What side?"

"Rocket's or the team's."

One of the trainers opened the door and stuck his head in, preventing her from commenting. "The hospital called. They have the X-rays on Mitchell and Rocket ready."

"Good. Please, let them know I'm on my way."

She didn't have time to return to her argument with Dalton. There were patients to consider. He'd been asked here to give a second opinion and he had. Now he was butting into what he didn't understand. It insulted her that he questioned her ability to put the players' health above the team's need.

Dalton was waiting with his new overcoat on and the bag of clothes she'd brought him by the time she'd stored her game clothes and picked up her purse. "I don't have time to drop you off at the Lodge. They are expecting me at the hospital."

"I already said I was going to the hospital with you."

Melanie started out the door. "Then you need to keep in mind that I'm the team doctor and I have the final say."

"I understand that. But, just so you know, I'll give my professional opinion as I see fit."

There was that tone she recognized from when they'd first met.

She wouldn't make any headway in this conversation so she kept walking toward her car. Snow had piled up on the windshield. "Would you hand me the scraper out of the glovebox?"

Dalton opened the passenger door. "I can do that—you go ahead and get in."

"Are you trying to tell me what to do again?"

His heavy sigh made a puff of fog in the cold air. "Melanie, I'm only trying to be helpful. Let's call a truce until we have both had some rest. We've had a busy, cold day and it's not over yet. Why don't we plan to fight this out tomorrow, if we must?" He found the scraper and started removing snow as if he wasn't still sore.

Melanie settled in the driver's seat and turned the heat up high. It had been an emotional day and if the truth be known she wanted nothing more than a hot bath and bed. But that would have to wait a few more hours.

She watched Dalton as he worked. Despite their recent argument, he had been a trooper and good help during the game. She'd been glad to have him on the field to confirm Mitchell's possible diagnosis and be there with Rocket. Still, she didn't like Dalton questioning her motives.

Hours later, Melanie pulled in front of the Lodge. She'd reviewed Mitchell's and Rocket's X-rays and visited both the men in their rooms. Neither was happy about having to stay overnight, but their wives and families were handling keeping them happy. Dalton had remained beside her the entire time. They had agreed on their earlier diagnosis of Mitchell's foot and were waiting on Rocket's MRI. The hospital had promised to notify her if anything changed during the night. She'd told the nurse she would be back first thing in the morning to check on them.

A groan coming from Dalton brought her attention back to the present.

"What's wrong?"

He pointed to a sign that read "No Water."

She couldn't leave him here. He deserved running water after the day they'd had.

He'd have to go home with her even if it strained her nerves to have him close all night.

"I guess you'd better come home with me."

"Don't sound so excited about the idea. I don't want to put you out."

"And I don't think I can take a long hot shower without feeling guilty if I leave you here. And I plan to have a long hot shower."

"So you're only being nice to me to ease your conscience?"

"Something like that."

He chuckled. "At least you're honest."

"I'll wait while you get the things you need."

"I don't have but one set of clothes really." He pulled at his shirt. "If you have a spare toothbrush I should be good."

She already knew he slept in the nude. Great. What was she getting herself into this time?

As she pulled out of the parking lot she said, "I hope they have the water on by tomorrow night because the Currents are having their Christmas party here."

Dalton was fairly sure that Melanie would have been perfectly happy to go home to an empty condo and have some time to herself. But he couldn't face a night without any water. He'd try to give her space and be as unobtrusive a guest as possible.

"Why don't you shower first? I have a few phone calls to make," she said as she removed her coat and hung it up on a peg just inside the door.

He put his jacket and the large bag with the extra clothes in it on a chair. "I can't take advantage of your hospitality by doing that. You have yours, then I'll get mine."

"When I get in I'm staying until the hot water is gone. If you want any, then you need to get it now." She walked into the kitchen.

"Okay, okay. I'll make it short."

Dalton tried to make it a quick shower but he stayed longer than he'd planned. The hot water felt so good, he couldn't bring himself not to enjoy it just a few more minutes. Forcing himself to get out, he toweled off. What was he going to wear?

He opened the door a crack and called, "Melanie!"

"Yes?" she answered a minute later from outside the door.

"I hate to ask you for anything more, but do you have any sweatpants or something else I can wear?" There was a moment of silence as if she were thinking.

"Wait a sec. I do have some old sweatpants somewhere that might fit you."

A moment later a hand thrust navy material through the crack. Dalton took it.

"Pass me your dirty clothes and I'll start them washing."

Scooping up the clothes he'd taken off, he handed them to her. Careful not to let her see him nude, he pulled on the sweatpants. They were smaller than he would have liked but at least he wouldn't be wearing just a towel.

Somehow her compassionate invitation tonight after their long day and fight made him resist applying any pressure to their wavering relationship. He wanted her to know that he respected her and appreciated her willingness to share her home. What he felt now was an odd emotion. One he wasn't sure he was comfortable with.

What if he let go? Really invested himself in a relationship? He couldn't do that—she'd eventually leave, as everyone he'd truly cared about had. It wasn't worth chancing the heartache.

He entered the living area to find Melanie standing behind the bar that separated the kitchen from the larger space. The TV was on and tuned to a channel with a digital fire.

"Nice fire," Dalton said.

Her eyes went wide when she saw him and her gaze settled on his bare chest long enough that he almost forgot his resolve to keep it simple between them.

She looked away. "I, uh, needed warming up. I thought it might help."

"I left you some hot water."

"Good. I'm on my way to use it all up."

Thoughts of Melanie taking a shower had him wanting to join her. But tonight wasn't the time to push. No matter how his need for her was growing. It was becoming more difficult every second because she only wore a housecoat. For a fleeting moment he questioned whether or not she had anything on under it.

"I'm sorry I didn't have a T-shirt large enough for you."

Did she mean that? Her gaze seemed to dart down to his chest and away again every few seconds. Her interest was an ego builder.

She held a mug up. "Would you like some tea or coffee? I'm out of hot chocolate. You hungry? Want a sandwich?"

"Thanks, a sandwich and tea would be great."

"The kettle is hot. Bags beside it. You'll find sandwich meat, cheese in the refrigerator and the bread is right here." She patted the bag sitting on the counter. "I'm going to get my shower. I've put bed things out on the sofa. Sorry I can't offer you your own bedroom."

She sounded so formal. Was she nervous?

"Melanie, I'm sorry I've been thrown in your lap like I have for the last few days. I know you probably thought you would pick me up from the airport and then be done with me. I do appreciate your efforts to make me comfortable."

"You're welcome, Dalton. I feel bad that you've been stuck here."

But he'd started to enjoy it. He hadn't realized how much he needed a vacation away from his demanding practice. He'd learned a few things in the past few days, had a story to tell and met Melanie. All in all, it hadn't been that bad. In fact, he couldn't remember laughing or smiling more.

Melanie headed for her bedroom. As she went in she said, "Good night."

Dalton watched the door close between them. Disappointment filled him. He wouldn't be sharing a meal with her. The ambience of the fire and a hot drink weren't the same when the woman you wanted to share it with was in another room.

He looked at the pile of bedclothes, then back at the door. The sound of water running reached his ears and a vision of Melanie standing under a stream of steamy water had the front of the stretch material he wore tightening. Dalton sighed. He wouldn't be getting much rest tonight.

Melanie purposely pulled on the oldest and most unrevealing pajamas she owned. She was still cold after her shower and the temptation to go to Dalton and ask him to hold her was too strong. She huddled in her bed, wishing for kisses from him that she knew from experience would heat her to the core.

He'd made no advances or even said anything that could be misconstrued as an innuendo since they'd entered her home. It was as if he were putting her at arm's length. Had their fight turned his interest sour?

It was disappointing to think he no longer wanted her. When he'd walked into the living room wearing those too-tight sweats, revealing more than they should have, and his wide chest and muscular arms bare, she almost couldn't breathe. If Dalton had given any indication of interest, she would have stepped into his arms and asked if she could join him in his shower.

But he hadn't and she didn't. It was best left alone anyway. He'd made it clear any relationship between them would be strictly physical, no long-term emotion. She closed her eyes, pulled herself into a ball and shivered. Hopefully, sleep would come. Exhaustion must have finally taken over because she woke to the faint sound of movement in the other room. Who was that? What time was it?

Dalton. Morning.

Well covered in her pajamas, she opened the door to her bedroom and stepped out. Dalton stood in front of the kitchen stove. Much to her disappointment, he was wearing his own clothes. There was no bare chest for her to feast on this morning. His shirt tail was out and he'd only closed two of the buttons across his abdomen. It was a nicer view than the sun rising over the falls. She'd like to enjoy the view every morning. A wish that wouldn't come true.

"Good morning, sleepyhead."

"Hey." She moved further into the room.

"I thought I was going to have to come wake you."

Melanie tingled at the idea. What would it be like to be awakened by Dalton? Would he kiss her awake? Nuzzle her neck? Run a hand along her leg? A shiver went through her. She had it bad.

"Is something wrong? You have a funny look on your face."

"No, no, nothing's wrong." She had to change the subject. "What're you doing back there?"

"I'm making us breakfast."

"And what will that be?"

"Scrambled eggs and toast." He pushed the spatula around the pan. "Should be ready in a minute."

"I'll dress, then. I have to get to the hospital and then check on the Christmas party preparations."

Dalton gave her a quizzical look. "Since when does a team doctor become involved in Christmas party decorations?"

"Coach is the general manager of the Currents, remember? He asked me to make sure everything is correctly done."

"Have you ever thought about saying no?" He pulled bread out of the toaster.

"Why would I?"

Dalton shook his head and murmured, "I guess you wouldn't."

She stepped closer to the bar. "What does that mean?"

"Breakfast is ready. Why don't we eat it while it's hot?" Dalton scooped eggs onto plates.

He hadn't answered her question. Did she really do her father's bidding? She'd always done as he asked. Had wanted to help as part of the team. She was only being a good daughter.

"So the plan for today is to go to the hospital and then back to the Lodge?" Dalton asked as he placed the plates on the table.

"Yes, but I can drop you by the Lodge first if you would like."

"I'd like to see Rocket's MRI."

Hopefully that wouldn't bring another round of disagreement between then. She didn't doubt that they both wanted the best for Rocket but she had other issues to consider. Dalton didn't understand that. Probably never would. "You are welcome at the team party, if you would like to come?"

"I don't think so. I don't like to crash parties."

Her fork stopped halfway to her mouth and she gave him a peeved look. "You're not crashing if I invite you. If it'll make you feel better you can come as my date."

He smirked. "Why, Melanie, are you asking me out?"

The man was making an effort at humor now?

She glared at him. "I'm trying to be polite but if you're going to be a smart aleck about it, then spend the night in your suite watching TV. The guys are fun to be around. After yesterday's game they'll be in high spirits. If nothing else, the food will be worth it. We use the best caterer in town."

"Since you put the invitation so sweetly, how can I resist? Yes, Melanie, I would love to be your date for the Christmas party."

He made it sound like there would be more to it than a friendly outing.

After breakfast they visited Mitchell and Rocket. Both were clamoring to see their discharge papers, which would put them out of the hospital in time for the party. The MRI showed that Rocket's knee had become marginally worse. The decision on whether or not to let him play would be made closer to the game. Finished there, Melanie drove them to the Lodge.

In the lobby Dalton asked, "What time do I need to be ready?"

"I have to be here at seven," Melanie said.

"Then I'll be waiting in the lobby for you."

"Okay." She headed down the hall to the ballroom.

Melanie stopped. The realization of what she'd done dawned on her. She had a date with Dalton! The evening pantsuit she'd planned to wear wouldn't do, especially after his remark about her fashion sense. Suddenly she wanted to show him just how much of a woman she was. And she knew just the dress to prove it.

She checked on the party preparations and was headed to the mall by just after lunchtime. Hopefully, no one had bought that red dress. With it being two days before Christmas, it took her far longer than she would have liked to find a parking space. She walked to and through the mall at a quick pace as if someone might snatch the dress off the mannequin minutes before she arrived. Breathing a sigh of relief when she saw it still in the window, she entered the store. She went straight to the counter and waited in line. When it was her turn, she asked to try the red dress on.

"It's the last one we have," the saleswoman said as they made their way to the front of the store.

Melanie's heart plummeted.

"What size are you?"

She told her.

"I think you just might be in luck." The saleswoman smiled as she took the mannequin down and began undressing her.

A few minutes later, Melanie had the dress on and was smoothing it over her hips. She stepped outside the dressing room to look in a mirror.

"It's perfect," the saleswoman breathed.

Melanie turned one way and then the other. Smiling, she said, "It is, isn't it?" She studied her reflection. A dress was only the start. She touched her hair.

"Big Christmas party to go to?" the saleswoman asked.

"Yes. And I know this may sound like a strange question, but can you suggest some place where I can have my hair and makeup done? This afternoon?" She hated the desperation in her voice. Did the fact she was out of her element show?

"Let me make a couple of calls. My sister works at a hair salon here in the mall. The department store at the end does free makeovers if you buy makeup. I have a friend that works there."

"Thank you so much."

Melanie had the dress off and paid for by the time the saleswoman had finished her calls.

She came to stand beside Melanie. "They are both expecting you. Ask for Heather at the salon and she will introduce you to Zoe for your makeup."

On impulse Melanie hugged her. "Thank you so much."

"Not a problem. My pleasure. Merry Christmas," she called as Melanie walked away with a spring in her step.

The salon was only a few stores down. Heather, a girl of about twentysomething with a blue streak in her hair, was waiting on her. "Mary said you were on your way. What would you like to have done?"

Melanie hesitated for a moment. "I'm not sure."

"Well, since you're going to a party, why don't we try a few different ideas and see what you like?"

Melanie nodded and followed. Two and a half hours later, she'd had a wash, trim and style. It was classic and perfect for her. She'd even had her nails and toes polished while having a facial. Already feeling like a different woman, it was now time for the makeup. That item was way out of her comfort zone.

Heather walked her down to the department store and introduced her to Zoe. In no time, she had Melanie in a chair and was showing her a makeup regimen. Forty-five minutes later, Melanie left with her eyes looking smoky and sensuous, her cheekbones accented, and her lips a pouty red. In her hand was a bag of makeup goodies to try on her own. She had never felt better about her looks.

On the way out of the store she passed the handbags. Unable to control herself, she bought a tiny sparkling red evening clutch and decided she also needed a pair of shoes.

As she drove home a ripple of insecurity raced through her. Would Dalton like her new look?

Dalton scanned the lobby for Melanie as he strolled down the stairs. Thankfully his ribs had improved each day. Now he could take a breath without a sharp pain. It was a good thing because the vest he wore would have hurt otherwise.

As Melanie had disappeared around the corner to see about the party room earlier, Dalton went over to Mark, the man behind the desk, and asked for assistance renting a tux. He had been very helpful.

Now Dalton was dressed in formal wear and he couldn't locate his date.

A woman wearing a red dress stood in front of the fire with her back to him. *Must be one of the players' wives or girlfriends.* They were known for having glamorous women on their arms.

He scanned the area again. Team members were filing though the door and the lobby was becoming more crowded by the minute. Where was Melanie? She wasn't usually late. Maybe she was busy in the ballroom. He was almost to the bottom of the stairs when the woman turned around. His breath caught. This time his heart, not his ribs, hurt. *Melanie.*

He'd never seen a more beautiful or alluring woman. Her hair was pulled up on the sides, accentuating her high cheekbones. Her eyes were skillfully highlighted and there was a tint of red on her lips. She looked nothing like the no-nonsense Melanie he'd become accustomed to. No woman in the nightclub scene in South Beach could have looked sexier.

His blood ran hot. She was *his* date tonight.

Melanie walked toward him in barely there shoes the same color as her dress. He almost missed the last tread of the stairs. Heaven help him, every fiber of his being screamed to forget the party and take her up to his suite.

"Hi, Dalton," she said in a soft, unsure voice.

"You look beautiful." He couldn't take his eyes off her.

"Expecting me to be in one of my masculine suits?" There was a teasing tone to her question.

"Well, actually, yes. But I find this a very nice change." Far too nice. He was in trouble. She tempted him already but as this gorgeous vamp, he was a goner.

"Thank you. Shall we go to the party?"

Dalton offered his arm. "Yes. I'll have the prettiest woman there on my arm. Just remember who brought you."

She giggled.

It was the first time he'd heard her do that and it reminded him of bells tinkling. He planned to make her giggle again. Soon.

They walked across the lobby. With the image of Melanie in that red dress, he might start seeing the Christmas season differently. As they passed the front entrance a large man who could only be a player said, "Is that you, Doc?"

"Hi, R.J.," Melanie said.

The player stared at her. "It really is you, Doc. You look great."

A touch of pink brightened Melanie's cheeks. She stood so close, Dalton felt her stiffen. He squeezed her hand resting on his arm to reassure her. He was afraid she might bolt. She'd been invisible for so long, this amount of attention had to make her insecure.

"Thank you, R.J."

Dalton led her away and around the corner, following the other players and their women, who were dressed in festive clothes, down a wide hallway. They entered the darkened ballroom that twinkled with white lights. A huge Christmas tree stood in one corner, decorated in Currents colors and with Currents ornaments. Surrounding the dance floor were tables set for a meal with flickering candles and greenery in the center.

"Merry Christmas, Juice," Melanie said.

A quizzical expression came over the player's face. "Wow, Doc. You look sexy." Shock followed and his gaze dropped. "Uh, I'm sorry, Doc, I shouldn't have said that."

She smiled. "It's okay, Juice. Thanks."

"Why don't we get some seats at a table?" Dalton suggested.

"Okay." She led him to a table close to the dance floor. Another couple was already seated there. Dalton held the chair for Melanie and she sank into it. The man Dalton recognized as one of the trainers leaned across the table and leered at Melanie. "Doc Mel. Is that you? You look great."

"Thanks, David. Hi, Katie." Melanie introduced Dalton to both of them, then said quietly to Dalton, "This is embarrassing. I never would've worn this dress if I had known it would cause such a scene. Maybe I need to go change."

"You will not! You're a beautiful woman and it won't hurt to remind some of these people you aren't one of the guys."

She looked at him and smiled. "No, it won't."

The players and staff kept stopping by and speaking to Melanie. She seemed to take their admiration more in her stride as they commented on her looks. About thirty minutes after he and Melanie had arrived at the party, Rocket and Mitchell limped in with arms locked and their wives at their sides. There was a round of applause. The men smiled broadly and bowed.

Soon after, Leon Hyde walked to the middle of the dance floor. One of the hotel staff handed him a microphone. The crowd quietened.

"Welcome, everyone. I'll make this short and sweet so we can get down to the important stuff. Eating and dancing. Thanks for the part you play on the Currents team. You've gone above and beyond this year and we still have two more playoff games and the Super Bowl to look forward to. If they are anything like yesterday's, the road will be an exciting one. Enjoy your holiday and come back ready to work. Merry Christmas, everyone."

The crowd clapped. Soon afterward, the room became loud with conversation and music. Dalton and Melanie, along with the other couples at their table, lined up at the buffet to get their dinner.

They were still there when Melanie's father stopped to speak to them. "Mel, did you check on Rocket's test today?" he asked.

Dalton couldn't believe it. He was the first male in the room who hadn't commented on Melanie's appearance. Didn't he ever really look at his daughter?

"Yes," Melanie said.

"Well?"

He seemed impatient for her to expand on the answer, as if he were in a hurry to move on.

"Rocket needs to rest for a couple of days. Then I'll re-evaluate him," Melanie hedged.

Her father didn't look pleased with her answer. "He has to play. The team needs him."

"I understand."

Dalton's hand tightened on the plate he held. Did her father always pressure Melanie like this? What kind of situation had Melanie grown up in? He hadn't had parents around but she had, yet was her father really there for her? Maybe their childhoods hadn't been that dissimilar after all. The difference was that Melanie stayed connected to people while he chose to keep anyone he might care about at a distance. Could he have done something different?

Leon Hyde extended his hand to Dalton. "Dr. Reynolds, it's nice to have you join us tonight."

"Thank you. I appreciate Melanie inviting me. Doesn't she look amazing?"

Her father regarded Dalton as if he were unsure about what to say, then look at Melanie and offered, "Very nice."

What was wrong with him? Couldn't he see that Melanie was a beautiful young woman? Efficient, intelligent, capable, but a woman nonetheless.

When her father's attention was pulled away by another man, Dalton put a hand at her waist and gave her a light hug. "I'm hungry, how about you?"

She nodded and gave him a smile that didn't reach her eyes.

Melanie had excused herself to go to the restroom. She was making her way back up the hall on her way to the ballroom. A group of players and their dates stood outside the door. There they were able to talk without screaming over the music. As she approached, one of the players with his back to her said, "Can you believe Dr. Mel?"

"You're not kidding. I had to do a double take. I don't think I've ever seen her legs," another player added.

One of the women leaned in. "Hank talks about Doc

Mel all the time. I always thought she was a he. After see-ing her tonight I might be jealous."

Hank put his hand around her waist and pulled the woman close. "Hey, you don't have to worry about that. Everyone thinks of Doc Mel as one of the guys."

One of the guys. That was what she'd been, growing up. She'd even dressed the part. As an adult that hadn't changed. She had no idea she'd receive such a reaction by just wearing a dress and spending a little more time on her appearance.

She moved by the group unnoticed and stepped inside the room. There she stood to the side, watching the activ-ity. The band had started playing and couples filled the dance floor. Other people talked in groups.

Dalton strolled toward her. He looked heart-stoppingly handsome in his tux.

"I've been looking for you."

That was all it took for her body to jumpstart to a hum.

"What's the most fascinating person in the room doing standing by herself?"

She gave him a bright smile. Dalton had always seen her as a woman. Even when he'd asked her about being a fe-male team doctor. She'd never been one of the guys to him.

"She's waiting on the most handsome man in the room to ask her to dance."

Even in the dim light she could see his gaze intensify at her flirting. He took her hand securely in his and led her to the floor. A slow song had just begun. Dalton's arms circled her waist. Melanie placed her hands at the nape of his neck. His hair brushed against her fingers.

His mouth came closer to her ear. "You've been the talk of the party."

She looked at him. "I'm not sure I like that."

"That's because you've been hiding the fact you're a woman for too long."

He was right. She wouldn't be doing that any longer. Starting tonight.

Melanie stepped closer to Dalton, bringing her body against his. He tensed, then his arms tightened. He was warm. His breath brushed against her hair. She inhaled. *Dalton.*

The dance floor was crowded yet the only person she saw or heard was him. They were in their own world.

He kissed her temple. Her fingers teased his hair. Dalton brought his hips to hers. The ridge of his swollen manhood clearly made his desire known.

The song ended. He said, "Melanie, I think we'd better sit the next one out."

"I don't want to." Her hand caressed his neck.

"Neither do I but I don't want to embarrass you. If I continue to hold you I'm going to start kissing you and I'm not going to stop."

Melanie liked the sound of that, but she did have a reputation and position to consider. "Okay."

They returned to their table. When they were seated Dalton took her hand and held it beneath the table. A number of the players brought their wives over to meet her.

The party started winding down none too soon for her.

"Do you have to stay and see about anything?" Dalton asked.

"I just need to check in with the person responsible for handling the party."

"When you are done, how about joining me for a view of the falls at midnight?"

She whispered in his ear, "Are you wooing me to your room, Dr. Reynolds?"

Dalton leaned back and captured her gaze. "Only if you want to be."

CHAPTER EIGHT

MELANIE'S FIST HESITATED for the second time in the air as she prepared to knock on Dalton's door. Just a few evenings earlier she'd spent the night in this suite. This time her hand shook as she went back and forth with indecision. If she stepped over the threshold she was afraid her life would change forever. Maybe she was making too much of the importance. After all, Dalton had been nothing but a gentleman. Why would he be any different now?

They could have a friendly cup of hot chocolate and look at the view. He'd mentioned nothing more. But the way he'd touched her earlier said he wanted everything she would give. If she took this chance, could she stand the hurt if he promised nothing more? What if she didn't go in? Would she always wonder what could have happened between them? Know that she could have taken a chance on love and hadn't because she was too afraid? Feared rejection too much?

Her skin heated. Dalton's desire for her while they were dancing had been obvious. Being wanted was stimulating. He'd made her feel like a woman. Something she didn't know she'd been missing until he'd come into her life. Even if she were to have just this one night, she wanted it with Dalton. As a female she had power and she wanted to use it, revel in it and savor it. Loving Dalton was worth the risk to her heart. All she could do was open it. It was up to him to accept what she was giving. If he didn't, then she had at least tried.

With head held high, she rapped on the door. It opened a second later as if Dalton were standing on the other side, waiting for her knock.

"Hi." She suddenly had a longing to flee. But she wouldn't. She wanted this. She wanted him.

Dalton had removed his jacket and taken off his tie. His vest hung loose. Could a man look sexier?

"Come in. Hot chocolate is almost ready. I was way-laid by Rocket when I crossed the lobby. Took me longer to get up here than I planned."

"Rocket does that sometimes." They were having a pleasant everyday conversation. What had she expected him to do? Pull her into the room, take her in his arms and slam the door? And to think she'd stood outside like a nervous virgin. She was over that. "I'm going to sit down and take these torture devices off my feet. If you don't mind?"

"Make yourself at home."

The only light burning in the room was the one over the bar area. She took a chair in front of the window. Sitting, she worked to release the strap of her shoe.

"Here, let me do that." Dalton placed two mugs on a nearby table and sat in the other chair. "Give me a foot."

Melanie swiveled the chair toward him and lifted a leg. He cupped his hand behind her ankle and rested it on his thigh. With the nimble fingers of a man who did delicate work for a living, he undid the strap.

"Other one."

His no-nonsense tone had her relaxing back against the chair. "Now this is the life. Beautiful view, hot chocolate on a snowy day and a man at my feet." She giggled. That sounded nothing like what she'd intended to say. Too suggestive.

Dalton's hand ran across the top of her foot, no longer encased. She looked at him. Their gazes met and held.

He brought her foot to his mouth and kissed her instep. Her breath caught. Her heartbeat went into overdrive. He reached for one of the mugs and handed it to her. "Just relax and let's enjoy the view."

She looked out at the falls but not for long. Her attention returned to Dalton. He was the better view. His profile in the dim light reminded her of a sculpture she'd seen in a European museum once. Her gaze followed the line of his forehead, along his nose, to his strong chin. She watched him so closely that she saw the movement of his mouth before he spoke.

"You're staring at me."

She looked at the falls. "No, I'm not."

"You were."

"Are you calling me a liar?"

Dalton wrapped both her legs with an arm and with his other hand he started to tickle the bottom of her feet.

"Stop!" She laughed.

"Admit you're a liar."

"I'm not." She chuckled again and tried to pull her legs away but he held on tighter, continuing to run his fingers over the bottom of her feet.

"You were staring at me. Say it—'I was staring at you.'" Dalton continued moving his fingers. She squirmed, causing her dress to inch up her thighs.

Melanie pulled at her hem, but it did little good. "I will not."

Dalton stopped and looked at her but still held her legs firmly. "You don't have to say it if you kiss me."

"That's blackmail!"

He cocked his head to the side and acted as if he was giving that statement a great deal of thought. "It is."

"You aren't worried about going to jail for coercion?"

He raised his chin and pursed his lips. His gaze captured hers. "You're not just any woman. So I'm willing to chance it."

"Okay, but you have to let me go."

"I don't think so." Dalton tugged her toward him. "I don't trust you." When she sat on the edge of the chair he reached an arm under her knees and one around her waist, then lifted her, bringing her to his lap. "Now it's time to pay for your lies."

He held her tightly.

Two could play this game. She shifted in his lap a couple of times, pulling on her dress as if she were trying to make herself decent. Done, she looked at him. His lips had thinned and his jaw was tight. He looked strained. She inwardly smiled.

Running her hands over his chest, she moved them up to his neckline. She slipped her fingers under the collar of his shirt. His intake of breath hissed. She brought her hands up to cup his face. Shifting again, her hip brushed against his hard length.

His eyelids lowered, hooding his eyes.

Melanie licked her lips. He groaned. She brought her face closer to his and whispered against his lips, "What was I supposed to say?"

Dalton's hands tightened on her waist as he growled, "Hell, it doesn't matter. Kiss me."

She did.

He gave her a moment of control before he seemed to lose his. His grip on her waist eased. One hand moved to the back of her neck. He pulled her lips more firmly into his. Melanie's hands went to his shoulders and gripped the fabric of his vest. Dalton eased the pressure as the tip of his tongue traced the seam of her lips. She opened her mouth and he thrust in.

Heat shot to her center. Blood pooled, hot and heavy. Her tongue met his with a confidence she'd never imagined. The man's loving was dangerous and exhilarating.

His lips left hers and moved to nuzzle behind her ear. She purred with pleasure. She offered him more access and

Dalton's lips traveled to her collarbone. There the tip of his tongue outlined its distance. His other hand cupped the top of her knee then went to the exposed expanse of her thigh. He lightly brushed her leg as his hand journeyed toward her hemline, teasing it before it went down her leg again.

Melanie turned her face and kissed him. Giving him lingering ones, then pressing her lips to his cheek before placing a kiss on his neck. Her fingers fiddled with the second button of his shirt until she had it open. She leaned over far enough for her lips to caress the skin visible in the V of his shirt.

He shifted, making her more aware of his length resting at her hip. His hand left her leg to cup her breast. She couldn't have stopped the sound of longing she made if she'd wanted to.

"Like my touch, do you?" His deep voice had taken on a raspy note.

His lips returned to hers as his hand slipped under the strap of her dress. When his fingers touched skin, she jerked.

"Shh," Dalton whispered against her lips. "You feel like warm silk."

Melanie relaxed. His hand at her waist slid up her back and pulled at the zipper. Slowly it came down as his lips found the ridge of her shoulder. With the zipper opened to the bottom of her shoulder blades, his hand returned to her neck. His fingertips tickled her skin as they trailed down her back. Melanie held her breath. Her skin was hot where he'd been, tingled where he touched and quivered in anticipation of his next move. She was a mass of sensations, all created by Dalton.

His mouth took hers in a honeyed kiss while his hand nudged her dress strap down her arm. She wore no bra, so his fingers were free to follow the same path back. Dalton's hand brushed the slope of her breast and rested there. His mouth left hers to place kisses across her cheek to her temple as his hand cupped her breast. The pad of his thumb teased her nipple until it stood rigid.

"Perfect," Dalton murmured. Using one of his fingers he started at the top of her breast and followed the slope down to circle her tip.

Melanie moaned as heat filled her and her core contracted.

"I want to see you." Dalton's fingers returned to the dress zipper and pulled it completely open. Using a hand on her shoulder, he leaned her back, supporting her across his arm. It left her open and vulnerable. Her arm went around his neck. He pushed her dress strap from her arm until her breasts were free.

His sharp intake of breath made the blood flow to her breasts, making them tingle with heaviness. She relished the fact that Dalton found pleasure in what he saw.

He cupped her breast again. As if weighing and committing it to memory, he fondled and caressed until she wriggled.

"Baby, you're killing me." He lifted his hip. "Have compassion."

Her hand rested over his bulge. "What's wrong?"

Dalton's fingers left her breast to remove her hand and place it in her lap.

"Not yet. I want to enjoy more of you."

His hand went to her breast again and lifted. She watched as his dark head came down to capture her nipple in his wet, warm mouth. Her eyes closed in pleasure as she soaked in every ounce of sensation.

Dalton's tongue swirled around her nipple, drawing and teasing until she writhed with need. Her hand flexed and released in his hair. Dalton growled low in his throat. He released her breast and kissed her neck. His tongue flicked out to taste her.

How much more of this could she take before she was consumed by the fire he created and stoked deep within her?

Dalton dragged her other strap down her arm until her dress gathered at her waist, leaving her breasts completely defenseless to his manipulations. His mouth found the neglected breast and made it feel as appreciated as he had the other one.

Melanie ran her hands through his hair, encouraging every tantalizing movement of his mouth. She had the fleeting thought that she should have been embarrassed by her wanton position both on him and in front of a public window, but all she could comprehended was her body's reaction to Dalton's ministrations. She'd never felt more free or more like a woman in her life.

One of Dalton's hands went to her thigh and slid under the skirt of her dress. His fingers skimmed her inner thigh and moved away. Slowly his hand moved up to the edge of her panties. One finger slipped under. It traced the line of her underwear toward her throbbing core. His mouth continued to do wondrously delicious things to her breast.

His finger made slow tormenting motions. Her muscles tensed. She parted her legs in invitation. He took it and grazed the lips of her opening. The ache curling in on itself became tighter. Panting in anticipation, she waited. Dalton was bolder this time. He pushed into her opening at the same time he tugged and swirled his tongue around her nipple.

Melanie arched like a bridge in his arms. With the power of the water flowing over the falls, she burst. For spectacular seconds she remained suspended in bliss before slowly returning to reality. Dalton was there to catch her. His arms circled her waist and his lips touched the top of her head.

Dalton had done many things in his life that made him feel successful but none had given him more satisfaction than watching Melanie come apart in his arms. He'd lifted his lips from her breast just in time to see her head roll back onto his shoulder, her eyes close and her lips part as she found her piece of heaven.

He'd been afraid that she wouldn't come to his room. Feared how badly he wanted her to. Felt foolish standing by the door like a kid waiting to get into a candy store. What was happening to him? He managed to keep women in their place, at a distance where he felt no real emotion, then along came Melanie. She had his feelings so twisted, he could think of nothing but her. He'd learned long ago that to care meant hurt. He was afraid things between them had already reached that stage. Could he walk away now? Would he want to?

He gazed at her, reclined in his lap, and smiled. She was stunning.

"Dalton, kiss me," Melanie whispered with her eyes shut and the sigh of release still on her lips.

He wouldn't turn that request down. His mouth found hers. She returned a tender kiss that made him even harder than he would have believed possible. If he didn't have her soon he would explode.

His look met hers. Placing a hand on her stomach, he made small circles over satiny skin. "You are so amazing."

"You're not half-bad yourself." One of her hands went to the opening in his shirt. She flattened her palm against his skin.

He loved her touch. Something that simple from her excited him.

"It's my turn."

"Oh?" He raised a brow.

She released another button of his shirt and ran a hand over his ribs. "Does it hurt much?"

He shook his head. "Only when I'm punched."

Melanie looked at him with troubled eyes. "I'm sorry I forgot." She undid another button. "Maybe I can make it up to you." The last button of his shirt slid out of its hole. She pushed the fabric away, exposing his stomach and ribs.

She pressed her lips to his skin. His muscles quivered in reaction.

"Does it hurt here?" Her mouth touched a rib. "Or here?" She found his skin again. Moving farther around to his side, her tongue darted out.

He flinched in reaction.

With a sound of satisfaction, Melanie said, "This must be the spot." Her hand dipped beneath his shirt and caressed his side while she continued to kiss him. Her breasts rested against his chest as she kissed his damaged body.

She looked up at him. "Better?"

"No," he ground out. "Because that isn't the part of me in pain."

"So where's your problem? Maybe I can kiss it and make it better," she said in a teasing tone.

The thought of that happening had Dalton ready to take her on the floor. Melanie deserved better than that, especially with it being the first time between them. He gave her a nudge from behind and she stood.

He wasted no time in standing also. "Heavens, woman, are you trying to kill me?"

She looked unsure, standing there with her dress circling her waist and her hair tousled.

He cupped her cheek and gave her a caressing kiss. "If you were to give me a kiss where I hurt it would be more than I could stand. Hold your hands above your head."

"Why?"

"Melanie, you can trust me."

Her arms went up. Dalton took the hem of her dress and pulled it off over her head. He dropped the material to the floor. His gaze met hers and held for a few seconds before it traveled down to her breasts. They were high and the nipples taut. Unable to resist, he reached out and took one in his palm. Releasing it, he watched it bounce gently.

He'd never been more fascinated. His gaze moved down to her barely there panties to follow the length of her legs. "You have gorgeous legs."

"Thank you."

"No, thank you for sharing them with me."

"You're starting to embarrass me."

"Why? I'm admiring you. You're beautiful and should be admired."

"That, and I'm standing here with almost no clothes on while you're still dressed."

He grinned and took her hand. "That problem's easily solved. Come with me."

Dalton led her across the living area to his bedroom. He turned off the light over the bar before he joined her. The only light came from the lamps shining around the falls. Shadows played over Melanie's body, making her appear otherworldly. Maybe she was. She'd certainly placed a spell on him.

He stopped beside the bed and released Melanie's hand. Taking hold of his vest and shirt, he started removing it.

"Let me help you." Melanie rested her palms on his chest and fanned them outward, pushing his clothing away. She continued over his shoulders and down his arms until the items were a pile on the floor. Coming closer, she reached for the button at his waist.

He stopped her movements with his hand over hers. She looked up at him with questioning eyes. His mouth came down to hers in a searing kiss she eagerly returned. His arms wrapped around her waist, bringing her against the ridge of his manhood. She rubbed against him. He wouldn't last much longer. He lifted her so that her feet didn't touch the floor and carried her the few feet to the bed.

Bending a knee, he laid her down on the comforter. Melanie looked at him with half-lidded eyes. She reminded him of a woman waiting on her lover in one of the old masters' paintings in the Louvre. All flesh, light and desire.

Dalton had every intention of being that lover.

His hands went to his pants button and released it and then the zipper in short order. He pushed his pants and underwear down at the same time. Stepping out of them, he stood.

Melanie's intake of breath made his chest swell. She liked what she saw. Just as she had when she'd been toweling him dry.

He moved to the bed and looked down at her. "Melanie, when I touch you again I will have to have you. I won't make any promise for the future. If you don't want that, it will kill me to let you go, but I will."

She leaned up. Taking his fingers, she tugged. "I want you. Even if it is just for tonight."

She understood him.

He came down over her, his mouth finding hers. She wrapped her arms around him and held him tight. As they kissed he pulled the covers back and then rolled to his side, taking her with him. He released her lips and said, "Crawl under."

As she brought her legs up, Dalton reached for her panties and pulled. "It's time for these to go."

Melanie lifted her hips and he slid the panties down and off her feet, throwing them to the floor. He flipped the covers over them and brought Melanie close. They lay facing each other. His gaze met hers. Her eyes were deep and luminous.

Unable to resist any longer, he glided a hand over the curve of her waist to her hip and across her behind. She blinked.

Melanie was perfect. He'd implied she should show off more of her body but now that it was his he didn't like the idea as much.

His? When had he started to think of her as belonging

to him? The second she'd so freely found her release in his arms. He hadn't planned this. Hadn't been looking for it, but he would embrace it while he could…while it lasted.

She ran her hand over his shoulder and down his bicep to his elbow. The back of her hand floated over his stomach and lower. One finger trailed the length of him. His need had become a gnawing animal within him.

He leaned away and found his pants on the floor. Pulling his wallet out, he located the foil square and opened it. After covering himself, he rolled back into Melanie's arms.

She lay on her back and moved between his legs. His mouth went to her tempting breasts before he kissed his way to her mouth. Her arms circled his neck.

Melanie whimpered and lifted her hips, bringing his erection into contact with her wet and waiting center. He requested she open her mouth for him and her tongue intertwined with his.

Dalton flexed his hips and entered her. He pulled back and Melanie's fingernails dug into his shoulders. She would leave marks that he would carry proudly. He lunged again. This time taking her completely. She stiffened. He pulled away but didn't leave her. She opened her legs wider and moved with him.

"Look at me, Melanie."

Her eyes flickered open.

He raised himself up on his hands and thrust again and again. He had to control her. Her body quivered, then tensed before she fell apart beneath him. Dalton leaned down and kissed her softly on the forehead. She would have no doubt who had brought her to ecstasy.

With another deep thrust, Dalton found his rapture as well. Maybe she had the control after all.

Melanie woke to the toasty heat of Dalton against her side. She snuggled closer. The arm around her waist tightened.

He'd awakened her during the early hours and made fast, hot, passionate love to her. Had she ever felt more alive?

She'd known other men, but none had such power over her with a single kiss or had created such a driving need to have him near. Mercy, the man knew how to love.

Love? That was what it had been with Dalton—love-making. She was in love with Dalton.

How had that happened? When he'd been so great with Rocket and Marcus? When he'd respected her boundaries? When he'd made his desire for her known more than once last night? It didn't matter when. It just mattered that it was a fact.

She loved him for standing up to her father, for knowing his own mind, for caring about sick children, for his sensitive care of Rocket—the list went on. But mostly she loved him because he saw her. The person. Not as a team member but as a woman, unique in her own right.

Melanie smiled to herself. Seconds later it slowly faded. She couldn't let him know. He'd made it clear that anything between them should have no emotional attachments. She was destined for heartache, but she would accept that when the time came.

She placed her arm over his at her waist and laced her fingers with his. Taking what she could while she could would have to be enough.

"Good morning, sleepyhead," he said in a raspy voice.

"I wouldn't be such a sleepyhead if someone hadn't woken me in the middle of the night."

His manhood, firm and long, stood against her hip. "I must not have done a good job if you are complaining about losing sleep."

"Now you're fishing for compliments."

He nuzzled her neck. "Maybe I need to convince you a little more that I rate praise."

"That's a good start." She turned to face him, interlinking her legs with his.

He chuckled, bringing a hand to her breast. "Why don't I start with…?"

Sometime later, with the sun streaming through the window and the roar of the falls outside, Melanie sat next to Dalton with a sheet pulled over her breasts, eating a grape off their room-service brunch. The sight of the sun was bittersweet. He would be leaving soon. He'd said nothing about how he felt about her. But he wouldn't; he'd made that clear. She was just a distraction while he was stuck in Niagara Falls. No way would she ruin what time she had with him by worrying about the future.

Dalton leaned over and kissed her bare shoulder. "What has you so deep in thought over here?"

"Just thinking that I've always wanted to wake up to this view of the falls."

"Have I been used?" he asked in an innocent tone.

"No more than you wanted to be."

He grinned. "I could have been used more."

"Now who is complaining?" She acted as if she were in a huff, planning to get out of bed.

Dalton took her hand, turned it over and kissed her palm. "I don't care the reason why—I'm just glad you're here."

Melanie melted. The man could charm a snake out of a basket without a flute.

"What do you have to do today?" Dalton placed their tray on the floor and rolled toward her. The sheet slid low over his hips.

He seemed unaffected while her body heated. Did he have any idea how irresistible he was? Drawing her eyes away so she could concentrate, she said, "Nothing but a little more cooking for Christmas dinner preparations. The

team has today, Christmas Eve and Christmas Day off. I
don't have to be back to work until Friday."

"Great. Then we can spend the day together." He tugged
at the sheet.

She held it tight against her. "That sounds nice to me."

"What would you like to do?"

The lump in her stomach eased. He wasn't talking about
leaving. "If it was summer I'd say we should go out on the
Maid of the Mist, but the river is too icy for that."

"Maid of the Mist?"

"The boat that goes out on the river and up close to
the falls."

"I like the view from here." Dalton looked out the picture window toward the falls, then back at her. "This view
is even better."

She leaned over and kissed his cheek. "I know what
I'd like to do but I don't know if you would enjoy it. And
it would be cold."

"What's that?"

"I'd like to go to the Festival of Lights and see the fireworks."

"That sounds like fun." Melanie's enthusiasm for the
season seemed to be rubbing off on him. "If I may borrow your brother's clothes again."

"Of course." She gave him a quick kiss and started out
of the bed, pulling the sheet with her.

"Where are you going?" He jerked the sheet out of her
hands.

"Hey, give that back!"

"No."

"Why not?"

"Because I want to admire you walking across the
room."

With great effort and heat on her cheeks, she strolled
to the bathroom. Inside, she closed the door and leaned
against it. Dalton was flipping her life over. She'd never

lain around in bed with a man, and certainly not naked. But he had insisted that they have breakfast in bed. To walk in front of him, or any other man, without clothes on was far beyond her comfort zone. What would he have her doing next?

Minutes later she was in the shower soaping her body when the glass door was pulled open. He stepped in.

"Dalton!" This was another first—taking a shower with a man—one that thrilled and terrified her.

"Melanie."

"I'll be through in a minute."

"I thought I could help."

"Help?"

"Scrub your back. Then maybe you could dry me off." He wiggled his eyebrows.

"I don't think—"

He grinned. "Melanie, in some ways you're so naive. Turn around."

She did as he asked. "Why do you call me Melanie when everyone else calls me Mel?"

"Because everyone else does call you Mel. Melanie is a pretty name. A feminine name. It suits you." With soap in hand, he moved it over her right shoulder.

She turned around to face him with a smile on her face. "Thank you. That's the nicest thing anyone has ever said to me."

He slipped his arms around her and pulled her against his wet, slick body. As Dalton's lips came toward hers he said, "I meant every word."

CHAPTER NINE

DALTON WAS STILL reliving and looking forward to more hot passionate minutes in a shower with Melanie as they walked along looking at the bright flashing and twinkling lights of the Festival of Lights. Melanie was like a child, pointing and running from one place to the next in her excitement. Just watching her made him smile.

Melanie had managed to slip under his barriers. Being around her was infectious. She had a wide-open heart that embraced the young and old, the large and the small, no matter how much she had going on in her life. She had managed in a few short days to make him see the pleasure in life, find humor. Most of all she'd made him discover what he could receive in return if he trusted himself enough to open up to someone.

Melanie had a happiness in her that didn't seem suppressed by her childhood. She saw joy in a child's smile when he received tickets to a football game, or when one of the players called hello, or even in preparing supper for her family who paid her little attention. How did she come away with such a positive outlook? Could he have tried harder to fit in at his foster homes?

He had to admit the festival was rather fascinating with its blocks' worth of buildings, animal shapes and plants all outlined in lights. A number of them were synchronized to music. Even the falls' water and mist had been lit so it appeared to turn different colors. The season was beginning to grow on him.

It was past time for him to go home, but he wasn't ready. The practice was closed for the holiday and he could stay until after Christmas without ruining his schedule. A long-distance relationship would be difficult to maintain. Would they even have a chance or would she tire of him not committing? Would she be willing to even try?

They strolled hand in hand as they looked at the displays and discussed them. At a small café they stopped in to warm themselves with hot chocolate and a cookie.

"I'd like to go up on the Ferris wheel," Melanie said after taking a sip of her drink.

Despite the cold and snow, he couldn't deny her anything. Plus the idea of huddling under a blanket, looking at the falls and stealing kisses from Melanie high up in their own private world had its appeal. He had it bad. "That sounds like fun."

She put her hand over his. "I think you'll be impressed."

"It'll be nice just to be with you."

She smiled, stood and started putting on her coat. "Then let's go."

He laughed. "You're more eager to go out into the cold than I am."

Melanie leaned down and gave him a quick kiss on the lips. "Who knows, if you're nice I might keep you warm."

His body fired at the thought. He stood. "Is that a promise?"

"Come on and see." She pulled on her knit cap.

Dalton enjoyed the banter between them. He'd never had that with another woman. Somehow Melanie brought out the impulsive side of him. That part of his personality had been buried until now.

They walked the two blocks to where the Ferris wheel turned. Each spoke and crossmember was decked out in white lights. After standing in a small line they were soon seated with a thick blanket over their laps and tucked around their feet. The chair rocked gently as they moved away from the ground. Melanie wrapped her arms around one of his, huddled close and laid her head on his shoulder. Dalton liked being the one she came to for comfort. Snowflakes drifted down around them. The lights grew smaller below them.

"Oh, look," Melanie whispered with amazement.

Dalton's gaze went to the falls, which were lit in the red and green of the season. "That is pretty amazing."

"I love it up here."

He kissed her.

"Hey, we better be careful—we might freeze together." She laughed.

"I wouldn't mind." He put his gloved hand over hers.

She clutched his arm tighter. "I wouldn't either."

They rode in silence for a few minutes, then Melanie said, "I can't believe tomorrow is Christmas Eve."

"I hadn't thought about it. I guess it is."

She shifted slightly and looked at him. "Would you like to come to dinner with my family tomorrow night?"

He'd never been very good at family celebrations. No real practice with them. He had no interest in being the odd man out. "I don't know. How would your family feel about me just showing up?"

"They'd be glad to have you. The more the merrier."

Something in him wanted to say yes while another part of him remained unsure. "Let me think about it. Christmas Eve isn't my favorite day of the year."

Melanie didn't say anything more for a few minutes. "Why not?"

"Because that's the day they took me from my mother and put me into foster care."

Her sniffle made him look at her. He brushed an icy tear from her cheek. "Hey, don't cry. Now, I have this time with you to replace that memory."

She kissed him and didn't say anything for a while. "Will you tell me about it?"

He didn't want to talk about his past but he was one hundred feet up. There was no easy way out.

"My parents were drug addicts." Her fingers pressed his arm in encouragement.

"My father went to jail a couple of months after I was born. When my mother went to prison, I didn't have anyone else to take care of me and I went into foster care. My foster parents tried, but I didn't fit in. I liked books. I was smarter than the other kids. And they knew it. I wasn't any good at what they liked to do. So I spent most of my time by myself."

"You said the other children liked to do things? Like what?"

"Like football, baseball, whatever game was in season."

"Oh. They must have made fun of the boy who read all the time."

"They did, but that's just how kids are. I understand that now. By the time I entered high school I was no longer that awkward kid anymore, but by then I was more interested in earning money to go to college than I was in playing sports."

"The kids called you names, didn't they? That's why you don't like nicknames."

Melanie was too smart. "It is."

A boom and the opening bulb of colored sparks raining down against the black sky drew their attention.

"Fireworks," Melanie said in awe.

Another round of light flashed in the night as they continued in a slow circle. Dalton placed his arm around Melanie's shoulders and pulled her close. They said nothing. Occasionally a soft "Oh…" came from her.

Talking about his past had been difficult, but sharing it with Melanie seemed to lift a weight from him. He appreciated the moments, just as he had when he'd spent time looking at the falls with her. Just being with Melanie seemed peaceful. He would miss that when she was no longer around. The thought saddened him more than he wished to admit.

He couldn't have planned it more perfectly when the grand finale of the fireworks went off as they came to the top of the wheel. Afterward they descended to unload. Offering Melanie his hand, she placed hers in his and stepped out.

"That was wonderful," she said. "Thanks for taking me up."

Dalton smiled. "You're right—it is fun. And I think you're the one who took me."

"You might be right. Uh, about dinner. Just know you're welcome. I'd like for you to be there, but only if you want to be. I can always bring you leftovers."

Dalton squeezed her hand. It might not be that bad to spend Christmas Eve with Melanie's family. They were an important part of her life. And she had become important to him.

They headed in the direction of where Melanie had parked the car.

"I didn't mean to put a damper on the evening by telling you my life's story," Dalton said after they had walked a block.

She took his arm again and hugged it close as they continued on. "No damper. I was just thinking about how much I would enjoy a hot shower."

"That sounds great. Mind if I join you?"

"I'd be mad if you didn't."

Melanie enjoyed their shower as much that night as she had earlier. Adding to the pleasure, she'd been toweled off by Dalton and she'd returned the favor. Now it was morning and she lay next to him, listening to his even breathing as he slept. He'd woken her in the early hours of the day and made love to her again. Instead of feeling tired, she felt invigorated. The man held a sweet power over her that she had no complaints about. Other than it wouldn't last.

A finger brushed the spot where her hip and leg joined. She looked at Dalton. His eyes were still closed but there was a hint of a smile around his lips. She made a move toward the edge of the bed. A hand clasped her wrist.

"Oh, no, you don't." Dalton tugged her back to him.

"I have to get going. I've dinner to finish. And I need to bake a cake."

"That can wait." He kissed the curve of her shoulder.

"I don't think so. I've already stayed in bed far too long." She tried to remove her hand from his grasp.

"What if I agree to help you? That would give you time for…" Dalton trailed off with a suggestive look at the bed.

"Don't tempt me."

His hand released her wrist and ran up her arm. "That's exactly what I'm trying to do."

"Well, as enticing as the invitation is, I'm going to have to take a rain check. I really must get moving."

"If I can't lure you into staying, then I guess I just need to go with you. Maybe if I help I can have a second helping of dressing."

Joy filled her. "You're coming to dinner?"

"Yes, thank you for the invitation."

She smiled widely. "Wonderful. I want my brothers and their families to meet you. I would have hated knowing you were spending Christmas Eve alone."

"Wouldn't you have stopped by afterwards?"

"Absolutely."

He gave her a long slow kiss. "That's nice to know."

Hours later she and Dalton unloaded food from her car and carried it into her father's house. He'd called while they were at her condo to tell her that he was at the office and would be there in time for dinner. Her brothers and their families would be arriving soon. One had flown in and the other two were driving. Dalton had questioned her about their arrival, but he'd said nothing about the fact the airport was open.

"Just put it down wherever you can find a spot in the kitchen," Melanie said over her shoulder as she carried the dressing into her father's house.

Melanie glanced around the living area as she walked through on her way to the kitchen. Her father had a simple ranch-style home that was large enough to hold the entire family. It was done in dark colors with pictures of her father with teams he'd coached on the wall. Autographed footballs set under glass in several places. Thanks to the maid that came weekly, the place looked clean and tidy.

Every home she'd lived in growing up had looked very similar to this one. There was a marked contrast between her condo and her father's. There was nothing in her place that said she was a sports fan. Her personal space was warm and feminine, right down to the yellow throw pillows on her sofa.

Dalton followed her in and put the turkey on the counter. "I'll go get the rest of the dishes while you get things together in here."

"Thanks, Dalton. You're a great help."

He was. She was so used to doing everything by herself she'd never realized how much work it was.

"No problem. By the way, did I tell you how nice you look?"

"Thank you." He knew how to make a woman feel like a woman. In and out of bed.

She didn't have much hanging in her closet that she considered superfeminine. After searching long enough that Dalton called from the other room that he'd loaded the car, she'd decided on a blouse in a silk fabric, a sweater with pearl buttons she'd pushed to the back of the closet and her most fashionable shoes. At Dalton's look of appreciation she had no doubt she'd made the right choices.

Melanie closed the refrigerator door after putting the congealed salad inside and walked over to him. Going up on her toes, she kissed him. "You look nice yourself."

His hands tightened around her waist. She stepped back despite the longing to move closer. "I still have a lot to do and you're a distraction."

Dalton let her go. "Then I guess you better give me a job so I won't be tempting you."

"Okay. You can see about getting the plates, napkins and silverware set up on the table. We'll eat buffet-style. There are far too many of us to fit around Coach's table."

"Why do you call your father Coach? You did that at the party." Dalton looked at her with an odd expression.

"I guess that's all I really ever heard him called, so I started doing it also."

"Your father was okay with that?"

"I think he likes it, actually."

"If I ever have kids, they will call me Dad or Daddy."

What she'd seen of his interaction with kids, he'd make an excellent daddy.

Over the next half an hour she gave Dalton directions, and he followed them to the letter. It would be her guess that he didn't often relinquish control to others. It impressed her that he was willing to do it for her.

The outside door burst open and a gush of freezing air announced her oldest brother, Mike. "Hey, Mel. How's it going?"

Melanie squealed and stopped what she was doing to hug him, his wife, Jeanie, and their three children. "Mike, Jeanie, kids, I'd like you to meet Dr. Dalton Reynolds."

"You can call me Dalton." He extended a hand to Mike.

"Nice to meet you, man," Mike said. "Mel, you don't even have the TV on. What about the game?"

Mike took a seat in front of the huge TV in the living

area. Jeanie came to the kitchen to help her, and the kids went to join their father. Dalton stood nearby with a be-mused look on his face. A few minutes later, her young-est brother, Jim, came in with his wife, Joan, and not far behind him was her middle brother, Luke.

"Hey, guys, doesn't Mel look great? I don't know if I've ever seen you dressed so…girly," Luke said.

She gave him a slap on the forearm, then circled his neck with her arms, giving him a hug. "Good to see you too. Thanks for the compliment, I think."

Dalton looked more uncomfortable as her family grew. Had she made a mistake by asking him to come? The sit-uation could quickly become overwhelming. While her sisters-in-law were busy in the kitchen, she slipped away to speak to him.

"Hey, how you holding up?" Melanie asked as she came up beside him where he leaned against the wall, observ-ing the men watching the football game.

"I'm fine."

"They can be a little, uh, overpowering."

He nodded as the entire male part of the family jumped up when something happened on the TV.

She slipped her hand into one of his and squeezed.

He smiled. "Yeah, but they seem like really nice guys. I'm glad I've gotten to meet them."

Melanie let go of Dalton's hand, not wanting her family to start asking twenty questions about their relationship. Melanie wasn't sure she could answer any of them. She had no idea where she and Dalton were headed. He'd said he only did short-term. If it was up to her she'd do what-ever it took to make it work between them. She'd had a full life before Dalton arrived, she thought, but now that he was in it, she wanted more. Her only hope was that when he left town, it wasn't for good.

About that time her father came through the door. Ev-eryone but her and Dalton lined up to either hug or shake hands and slap each other's backs in welcome. With that done, her father stepped over to them. "Glad you could make it, Dr. Reynolds. Mel, I guess you have everything ready."

"Yes. It'll be on the table at halftime."

"Good." He went to join the others, who had returned to the game.

Dalton looked at her in astonishment. "Do you always plan meals around football games?"

"Not always. But this year there's a special Christmas Eve game on." Why did she feel as if she needed to apologize? She looked at her family. Was their world too wrapped up in the sport?

One of her sisters-in-law insisted they turned the TV off completely while they had their meal. There was moaning and groaning, but when all the grown females agreed the TV went black.

While she and Dalton were standing in line waiting to serve their plates, Mike said, "So, Dalton, you're the guy our sister spent the night with?"

"Mike!" Melanie shrieked in embarrassment. Did he know about the past few days?

Dalton looked at her and grinned. "Yes, that was me."

"Dalton!"

He shrugged his shoulders. "Hey, I'm just telling the truth."

Mike laughed.

"Yeah, Dad told us about you getting hit by Juice. I've played against him and I'm impressed you're out of hospital," Jim said with a chuckle.

"Thanks for taking care of our kid sister." Luke wrapped an arm across her shoulders and squeezed. "We couldn't do without her."

"You're welcome," Dalton said. "She is pretty special."

"We would agree with that," said her brother from the other side of the table.

She and Dalton found places to sit beside each other on one of the two large couches. They held their plates in their laps. What room there was at the dining room table was given to the children.

"So, Mel, you going to sign off on Rocket playing on Sunday?" Jim asked.

She sat close enough to Dalton to feel him tense. Why had Jim brought up that subject?

"We—" she indicated Dalton "—still need to assess him again."

Her father returned from refilling his plate. "Mel's a team player. She'll see that Rocket is on the field."

Melanie felt Dalton's gaze on her, but she said nothing. She shifted on the couch cushion. Was she a team player anymore? Had she ever been? Maybe she'd just been playing the part her father wanted her to?

With the meal over as well as the game, everyone gathered around the tree. Presents were distributed. Melanie watched the look of shock on his face when her niece said, "Dalton. Who's Dalton?"

Her mother said, "Dr. Reynolds."

"Oh." Her niece carried the small present to Dalton.

He looked at Melanie.

She smiled. "Everyone gets a present under our tree."

"But I didn't—"

"That doesn't matter. Open it."

Dalton pulled the paper off and lifted the top. He reached down and picked up the lapel pin depicting the waterfall with "Currents" written across it. A smile spread across his face.

"Something to remember us by," Melanie said. She really meant *remember her by.*

"Thank you. I can't tell you the last time I got a Christmas present. I'm sorry I didn't get you anything."

She leaned close. "I'll take a kiss later."

He captured her gaze. "You can count on that."

Soon after the presents were all opened, her brothers and their families left to stay in rooms at the Lodge. She and Dalton were loading the last of the dishes into her car when her father said, "Mel, I've called a press conference for the day after tomorrow at nine a.m. I'll expect you to be there to reassure everyone about Rocket."

"Coach, I still need to reevaluate him." She wished she'd sounded firmer.

"Then have it done before the press conference."

"Mr. Hyde, with all due respect, I don't think it's in Rocket's best interest to even consider playing."

"Dr. Reynolds, I appreciate you coming all the way up here and I'm sorry that you've had such a difficult and long stay, but you've given your opinion. Mel has the final say as the team doctor."

When Dalton started to say more she placed a hand on his. "It's Christmas Eve. Let's not get into this tonight. Day after tomorrow will be soon enough."

Her father said, "Mel, I've taught you what's expected when you're a member of a team."

Melanie knew that all too well. *Do what's best for the team.* She resented the pressure he was applying. Was uncomfortable with Dalton seeing how her father treated her. Maybe she should be a team player and go along. She always had before. No, she couldn't face Dalton or herself if she didn't do what was best for Rocket. Disappointing her father would be hard, but lowering her medical and personal standards would be worse.

She kissed her father on the cheek. "Merry Christmas, Coach." The words were flat, even to her own ears.

Dalton said little on their drive back to her house and neither did she. The proverbial two hundred and fifty—pound football player in the car kept them quiet. That was pressure of its own. Now she felt as if her father was pulling her one way and Dalton the other. They carried in the dishes with few words spoken. Melanie went to the kitchen and started putting leftovers into storage containers.

"I'm glad you came tonight," she said as she cleaned out the dressing pan. She meant it, but would he ever be the kind of guy that would enjoy going to her family's get-togethers? "I know my family can be a bit much."

Dalton moved away from where he stood looking at her Christmas tree and came to stand on the other side of the bar facing her. "I'm glad I went. I better understand you."

She met his gaze. "How's that?"

He shrugged. "Just that now I know why you work with a professional football team but spend your days off at a children's hospital. Or why you were so surprised at the party the other night that they thought you are an attractive woman. And why you are letting your father manipulate you into doing something you know isn't right."

"My father is not manipulating me."

"You don't call what he said tonight manipulation? Your reaction was to say nothing. Classic control method. You didn't even tell him there's a good chance that Rocket will not play."

"I don't know that for sure." She was starting to get annoyed.

Dalton's chin went down and he gave her a look that said, *You have to be kidding.* "Oh, come on Melanie. You do too. You know as well as I do that it isn't in Rocket's best interest to play. You called me in as an expert when you already knew he shouldn't play. But you are letting you father push you into believing differently. It's more important to win than for a man to maintain his health and mobility. What it boils down to is, you want to make your father happy so he'll notice you."

"How dare you?" The spoon she held fell from her fingers and clinked on the floor. She ignored it. Anger fired in her chest.

"I dare because…"

"Because why?"

"It doesn't matter. It doesn't take much to see that your father has always treated you as one of the guys in your family instead of a daughter who needed a father's attention. That extends to your professional life and now he sees you as a puppet he can manipulate."

That was how her ex-boyfriend had treated her when he was trying to get a job with her father. She'd been his puppet for months. When he didn't get what he wanted he threw her away. Her fingers gripped the edge of the counter. "That's not true!"

"I disagree."

She hated the calm smug way he spoke to her.

"If I was willing to bet, I'd put my money on it that it wasn't your idea to become the team doctor."

He was right. It hadn't been. She wanted to be a pediatrician.

"I'm right. I can see it on your face. You care too much about what your family expects. Your father is so focused on football he hardly recognizes you as the wonderful, remarkable woman you are. In many ways you're guilty of fostering that. You wanted to be a pediatrician but did what would keep you included by the family and noticed by your father. You're a caring and bright doctor with a large heart, and you are all woman when you let it show. Stand up to your father. Stand up for Rocket and yourself."

Dalton watched as Melanie stood straighter. She glared at him. The wild look in her eyes said he'd pushed too far. He'd almost told her he cared for her, but if she rejected him, he didn't know if he'd recover. Having gone years without letting someone have that kind of power, he couldn't risk doing so now.

"How dare you presume to tell me how a family works? You know nothing about family dynamics."

He flinched. She was cutting deep.

"What qualifies you to judge mine?" she all but spat.

He held up a soothing hand. "You're right—I don't know about families. But what I do know is medicine and knees. If you let your father or anyone else on the Currents staff pressure Rocket to play on Sunday, they are wrong. He could damage his leg permanently."

"But we don't know that for sure."

"I do."

"How, Dalton? Because you're the go-to man for leg injuries? Because you are all-knowing and all-seeing. You're not any better than you think my father is. You want to oversee every decision. Be the final word. You're so used to being right or having the ultimate say that you can't stand the thought that someone might disagree with you or want to do it differently."

"I'll have you know that I always put my patients first." Dalton stepped back. He was starting to lose control of the conversation and Melanie.

"And I always put my players first. Still, it's not as cut-and-dried as you think it is. You have a practice where you're the king of the mountain. You've spent all your life standing alone. Trying to prove to yourself and others that you're worthy of being wanted, or asked to join the team. Even when you could have been chosen you remain by yourself. You are so afraid of being rejected you are scared to let go. So don't tell me about what I should do when you have no idea what it's like to carry so many others on one decision."

What she said smarted.

"I think I should leave before either one of us says something they might regret."

"That figures."

"What?"

"Running and hiding when it gets too hard. Anytime you lose the upper hand or feel the situation slipping out of your control you leave. Is that what you have been doing all your adult life? That way you don't have to worry about ever feeling like you did as a kid. Of all people, you're the one telling me to stand up to my father. But you haven't left your past behind. It follows you like a chain with a ball attached. You even made it clear that what was between us would be only temporary because you were afraid you might feel too much. Might have to stay in one place and commit.

"You're highly successful, top in your field, yet you still think like the little boy who wasn't picked to play ball. You fear that anyone you have a real connection with will turn you away. Not want you. No one likes to be rejected. I certainly didn't."

"How is that?"

She glared at him. "My old boyfriend used me to get a job with my father. When I said I wouldn't help him, he dumped me. Everyone gets rejected, so don't think you are so special in that regard. How others feel and act isn't under your control. You're afraid they will disappoint you or hurt you. You don't give them a chance to show you anything different. It's time to trust you're worth having."

Now she was starting to throw mud. "Don't take the high road here, Melanie. I may have to be in control because of my past, but you're controlled in the present. I'm not sure one is better than the other. You think I can't say what I feel, but I can." He pointed to her and back to himself. "There is something special between us."

Her eyes widened.

"Don't act so surprised. You know as well as I do that what has happened over the last few days is rare between a couple. I wanted us to figure out how to make it work. Now I think that's not possible until you can make a decision for yourself, out from under you father's thumb."

"And I think you need to revisit your past so you can face the future. Learn to be a part of a relationship wholeheartedly. Find value in yourself, not through your profession."

Dalton shook his head. "I'm sorry things ended this way between us. It's not what I had hoped for. I'll call for a taxi and wait at the store down the street."

It took a few seconds before she sighed, then said, "Don't do that. I'll drive you to the Lodge." She walked to the coatrack.

He didn't argue. The idea of walking down the street in the cold did nothing to improve his spirits. They rode in silence to the Lodge. Dalton was afraid to say more for fear he'd make the situation worse. Melanie pulled to a stop at the front door.

He climbed out. "Goodbye, Melanie."

"Goodbye, Dalton."

CHAPTER TEN

MELANIE TOOK A deep breath and adjusted the collar of her shirt. Looking into the mirror in the bathroom of her office one more time, she saw only the red rimming her eyes. Hopefully the cameras wouldn't be on her that long. She had the press conference to get through, then she would have a few days to compose herself before the game. And she would collect herself—she had to.

It had been the longest drive of her life back to her condo after dropping Dalton off. Back home, she'd not even stopped to finish storing the leftovers from dinner. Instead, she'd gone straight to her bathroom and turned on the shower. Climbing in, she'd let her tears flow with the water until it was cold.

How had things turned so ugly between her and Dalton? She'd never spoken to another person with such venom before. Why him? Because she cared so much.

She'd called the Lodge the next morning, asking for him. Mark was on duty and he told her that Dalton had already left for the airport.

Christmas morning. Merry Christmas. He must have been really angry with her.

Melanie had spent the rest of the day vacillating between wallowing in pity and eating every piece of candy she could find. By the middle of the afternoon, she'd called her father and told him she wouldn't be by, but would see him at the press conference. With her brothers in town, she wouldn't be missed.

She went over her conversation with Dalton again and again. Their upbringings had been miles apart—him by himself and her with people to answer to all the time. They were too different to understand each other. But they had no trouble communicating in bed. So much so that she missed him with a pain that was almost breathtaking. Surely with time that would ease. If it didn't, she had no idea how she would survive.

Now it was time to put on a happy face to the sports world. She'd done a few press conferences but they still weren't her idea of fun.

A knock came at her office door. "Hey, Doc, Mr. Hyde sent me down to tell you it's time."

"Thanks, I'm on my way."

Her father was eager for this press conference to go his way. There hadn't been time to do new tests on Rocket. She had spoken to him earlier that morning and he'd said his leg felt fine.

Ten minutes later Melanie was sitting at a table in front of the press with her father, Rocket and Coach Rizzo.

Her father started the conference by making a statement about his hopes for victory on Sunday. "And now we will take a few questions."

The people in the room all started talking at once. "Dr. Hyde, Dr. Hyde."

Her father recognized the man.

Melanie forced a smile. "Yes?"

"What is your professional opinion regarding Rocket playing this Sunday?"

She took a deep breath. "Rocket has been resting his leg. Closer to game day, I will put him through a battery of tests and make the final decision about whether he plays or not."

Her father leaned toward the microphone, "All plans

are for Rocket to be on the field Sunday. I'm sure you agree, Dr. Hyde."

She couldn't believe that her father was now putting words in her mouth on national TV. Could he undermine her professionally any more effectively?

It seemed to take forever for the press conference to end. She spoke to Rocket, telling him she wanted to see him in her exam room in thirty minutes, and she left.

Dalton had been right. She was letting her father push her around about Rocket and that had to stop today. Back in her office, she called her father's secretary and asked to see him that afternoon.

Rocket showed up on time and she did her exam. She sent him for an X-ray and told him to spend some time with the trainers working on the machines. Rocket seemed upbeat and talked of nothing but playing in the game. Tension and excitement filled the building with everyone in high spirits about the Currents' chances of winning.

At the time slot Melanie had been given, she arrived at her father's office. She was announced over the phone by his secretary. Her father waved her into a chair in front of his desk as he continued his phone conversation. Just like at his home, football memorabilia filled every shelf. There were a few old pictures of her brother's children but nothing of the entire family together or of her.

A few minutes after she'd arrived, he hung up and said, "Mel, I think the press conference went well."

"Coach, that's what I want to talk to you about."

"Is something wrong?"

"I wish you hadn't said Rocket would be playing on Sunday. It isn't a sure thing. It's my job to make those determinations. I would appreciate it if you wouldn't put words into my mouth."

Her father leaned forward in his chair and gave her a pointed look. "And my job is to keep the franchise making money. Part of that is putting the correct spin on the situation. I want Rocket on the field. Give him steroid shots, pain relievers—I don't care what. But it's your job to see that he plays."

"That's where you are wrong, Coach. It's my job to see that the players remain in good health. That their lives now and later aren't put in jeopardy. I can't stand by while anything different happens."

"You will do as you are told."

Dalton had called it. She'd been so caught up in being noticed by her father she'd compromised who she was. She blinked. But no more. She would no longer be anyone's puppet. It was time for a drastic change. One that was overdue.

"Father—" at her use of that unfamiliar address he cocked his head and gave her a questioning look "—I won't."

"Mel—"

"It's Melanie."

"What has gotten into you?"

"Nothing that shouldn't have happened sooner. I won't agree to Rocket playing on Sunday or any other Sunday until next season. His leg will not improve enough in the next few days for him to play. I'm not going to sign off on him. Dr. Reynolds was right and I should have agreed with him when he gave his opinion. The team will have to win without Rocket."

"Mel, you are part of the team. You need to act like a team member."

"No, Father, I need to do what is best for Rocket and that is for him not to play."

Her father stood. "This is more than just about one person."

"That's where you are wrong. It is about a person. You never have seen the individual. It has always been about the team—in your professional and private life. I no longer want to be a part of a team. I want to be your daughter.

That is all. I love medicine but I have always wanted to work with kids. I'm thankful for all you have done for me but it's time for Melanie Hyde to be herself. I'll be turning in my resignation after the season is over."

"Mel, I think you should give this more thought." His voice rose.

"No, sir, I think that's the problem. I've been using my head instead of my heart for too long. I'm going with my heart now."

"Mel—"

"Melanie, please."

Her father's face had turned red. "Melanie, we'll talk again when you're more rational."

"I won't be changing my mind about Rocket or leaving. I love you, Father, but it's time for me to live the life I choose. Not the one chosen for me."

Her father wore a perplexed look on his face as if he hadn't comprehended a word she'd said. His phone rang and, to his credit, he paused a second before he answered it. As he did, she left the office.

Dalton flapped the file he'd been reviewing down on his desk. It had been two weeks since he'd left Niagara Falls. It was a new year but it hadn't been a good one. He missed Melanie to a degree he would have never thought possible. It was almost a physical pain that didn't seem to ease.

He fingered the file he'd just put down. It was Josey Woods's—one of the patients he and Melanie had seen on the day they went to the children's hospital. His colleague had spoken to him about Josey being a good candidate for a new procedure they were doing on children her age with long-term bone malformation. The only complication was her recent chemo. When she was far enough out, they would bring her in for the surgery. Josey was just one more reminder of Melanie. As if he needed one.

As soon as he had returned to the Lodge, he'd called

to see if he could get a flight home. There had been one early the next morning. More than once he'd started to call Melanie but had pushed Off on his phone. As he'd watched her interaction with her family he'd felt her pain that they took her for granted. Worse than that—how could a man pretend to care about Melanie to get to her father? She deserved better. He was furious on her behalf.

What if he and Melanie had tried to make it work? Their backgrounds were so far apart, would they have made it a month, six, a year? Would he have ever fit into her family? Yet he and Melanie had been so close. Their bodies in sync with each other.

She'd accused him of running away. Maybe he had but he needed a chance to think. Give her space as well. It was time he went home anyway. He'd opened himself to her more than he had to anyone in his life. Even gone so far as to tell her he cared about her on a level he didn't clearly understand at the time. He'd returned to the world he knew and understood, yet he was out of control. Something was missing. That something was Melanie.

He'd unfastened the part of his heart he'd guarded so carefully for so many years and let her in. She'd ended up capturing his entire heart and he'd left it behind in Niagara Falls with her. He couldn't deny it. He'd fallen in love with Melanie.

But even that knowledge didn't make his life any better—if anything, it made it worse. He'd told her it was up to her to come to him. She had to break away from her father. See herself as Dalton did. As a strong woman who was special in her own right, not because she was just part of a group. It was for her own good. He only hoped she realized it before the pain of losing her killed him.

He'd watched the game on Sunday for two reasons. One—to see if Melanie agreed to let Rocket play. And the other—to see if he could catch a glimpse of her. To his displeasure, he hadn't seen Melanie. To his frustration and disappointment, Rocket was dressed in his game uniform ready to play. The sports announcers said that Rocket was being held in reserve in case he was needed. If the team fell behind, he'd be sent in. Because the Currents were winning for most of the game, Rocket never had a chance to play. The announcer went on to say that they were saving Rocket's leg for the Super Bowl. Still, Melanie must have given her okay for him to play or he wouldn't have been on the sideline in his uniform. Nothing had changed.

The Currents won the game, but Dalton didn't see it as a victory.

Now, he looked out the window of his second-floor office at the top of a palm tree that blew gently in the south Florida breeze. A statement that Melanie had made during their argument continued to haunt him. She'd said he needed to face his past, make peace with it so he could understand relationships. Was that what he'd been doing all these years—hiding from people? If his affair with Melanie was an example, hiding might have been a good thing. If you let go and showed weakness you could get hurt.

In his adult life he'd made sure he was always in control. While he'd been in Niagara he'd not had that luxury and he'd never been happier. Did he want to go back to being the old Dalton? Now that he knew what it felt like to have someone care about him, and to care about them in return, he wasn't so sure.

If Melanie came looking for him, would he be the man she wanted if he didn't reconcile with his past?

Three days later he turned right into the street where he'd lived when he was ten and eleven. He'd already visited two places of the five where he had lived as a child. One of the houses had been boarded up and the other had a different family living in it. He hadn't expected to speak to anyone when he'd started his road trip northward to a town in central Florida, but something pushed him to knock on the door.

Dalton drove slowly down the street, watching for the all-too-familiar yellow house in the middle of the row. He pulled to the curb across from it. Toys still littered the yard. There was a car in the drive. Someone must be home. What was gone was the empty lot next door where everyone had gathered to play. Did his foster parents still live here?

He climbed out of his car and started toward the house. Some of his hardest years had been spent here. This was where he'd lived when he'd made up his mind he would be a doctor, make something of himself and leave who he had been behind. He'd managed to do that until Melanie came into his life.

Standing on the porch, he knocked on the screen door. He waited a few seconds and knocked again. The shuffle of feet came from inside and then the door was open a crack.

"Can I help you?"

"Mrs. Richie?" Dalton asked, peering through the screen to see the old woman's features.

"Yes."

"I don't know if you remember me, but I'm Dalton Reynolds. I lived here for a while. I was one of your foster kids."

She pushed the screen door open. "Dalton Reynolds! Of course I remember you. How're you doing?"

"I'm fine. I'm a doctor in Miami."

"Do tell. But I'm not surprised. I always knew you would make it. You were a tough one. Come in and tell me about yourself."

She turned and headed down the hall he remembered as longer and wider. Not given a choice, he followed her to the kitchen. It hadn't changed much. Some of the appliances looked new, but otherwise it was the same.

"Have a seat, Dalton. I'll get us some iced tea." She went to the cabinet and pulled two glasses out.

Dalton sat in the chair he had as a child. It creaked, just as it had then.

Mrs. Richie walked to the refrigerator, removed a pitcher and filled the glasses. She came to the table and placed one in front of him and the other down next to the chair she eased into.

"It's nice to hear you're so successful." She took a sip of tea.

"Why? You didn't think I would be?"

"Heavens, no. I could see you were smart. You made good grades even though you were so unhappy. You didn't let that stop you."

He met her look. "You knew I was miserable?"

"I could tell from our talks you were unhappy. I knew how the other kids treated you."

"Why didn't you do something to stop it?"

"Because it would have only made it worse. If I had stepped in for you every time it would have been harder for you when I wasn't around. I had confidence you would find a way around it. You did. You concentrated on being a good student."

"I read all the time."

"You did. I knew you were trying to escape, so I saw to it that there were plenty of books around on your level and above."

And there had been. Dalton had never questioned why there was a steady stream of books available to him. Or why Mrs. Richie loaded everyone up to go to the library every Saturday when he was the only one willing. In her own way she had given him a wonderful gift.

"But I didn't have any friends."

"That's why I suggested to your caseworker that you

might be better off moving to another home. I could see things were getting hard for you around this neighborhood."

He'd seen the move as a betrayal when she'd been trying to help him. Life had been better for him in the next home. He'd stayed there until he'd graduated from high school. "Thank you, Mrs. Richie."

"You're welcome. Now tell me about your life. Do you have a wife and children?"

"No. But I hope to soon." Dalton spent the next few minutes telling her about himself. When he left, she made him promise to keep in touch, even if it was a yearly Christmas card.

"You're one of the success stories, Dalton. Be proud of yourself. I am."

Dalton wasn't proud of the way he'd left things with Melanie. That he planned to remedy right away.

Melanie didn't stay for the Super Bowl celebration. The Currents had won by a wide margin. Without Rocket. She'd already cleaned out her office and said her goodbyes. She would miss the players and staff. They had become like family, but it was time to move on and find another family. With any luck, maybe create one of her own.

She smiled as she stepped out of Miami Airport and the heat of the sun touched her face. Just a few hours ago she'd been knee-deep in snow. She was trading that for sand. Pulling the strap of her small bag over her shoulder, Melanie raised her hand for a taxi.

Two hours later, she stood in front of what she hoped was the door to Dalton's apartment. It had taken some web surfing, phone calls to colleagues and one heart-to-heart with Dalton's secretary to find out the address, but she hadn't given up. She just hoped another woman didn't answer the door.

Pushing the doorbell, she waited. Nothing. Pushing it

again, she listened for footsteps. None. Fumbling around in her purse, she found her business card and a pen. On the back of the card she wrote: "Came for that visit. I'm at the beach."

She took the elevator down from the penthouse floor and crossed the street to the beach. Despite it being the middle of January, there were a number of people enjoying the water. Pulling her new towel out of her new beach bag, she laid it out on the sand near the water. She removed her cover-up and sat on the towel. It was a beautiful spot.

Looking over her shoulder, she searched what she believed were Dalton's windows for movement and saw none. Her nerves were getting the better of her. Would he be glad to see her? Worse, ignore her note? She just had to hope that she hadn't been imagining what had happened between them in Niagara. He had said he cared. Surely that hadn't changed in a month.

It was a workday, so he probably wouldn't be home for another two or three hours. She could enjoy the beach for a while and worry later. Pulling her bag to her, she reached in and brought out a romance novel she'd bought in the airport. It would have a happy ending even if she didn't get hers.

Melanie woke with a sense that someone sat beside her. She opened one lid to see a shadow across the bottom half of her body. It was a big person. She opened both eyes. It was a man, but she was looking into the sun and she couldn't see his face but she did recognize those shoulders.

"Dalton..."

"What are you doing here, Melanie?" He didn't sound excited to see her.

She sat up. "You said I should come visit."

He wore a shirt with a too-heavy-for-the-climate sweater over it and long pants, socks and boots. The man had a serious problem with wardrobe decisions.

"No, I meant here on the beach. You're burnt. You

should know better than to stay in the sun too long when you're not used to it."

Melanie looked down at the tops of her feet. She would be unhappy soon as the sunburn set in.

Dalton stood in the shifting sand with all the grace that she'd remembered him having. He offered her his hand. "Come on—let's go get some aloe on you before you start hurting."

She took his hand and he helped her stand.

He handed her the cover-up. "Pull this on while I put the rest of your stuff in your bag." He picked up her book and raised a brow before placing it inside.

Melanie slipped on the oversize T-shirt. Dalton didn't seem pleased or upset to see her. She wasn't sure how to take that.

He carried her bag as they walked across the sand toward his place. Not once had he touched her. Fear started to seep in that he never would again. He was being too civil after all the harsh words she'd said. They seemed never to be on the same wavelength except in bed. Even now she was half-clothed and he was dressed as if he was headed to snow country. *Snow country.* Had he been coming to see her?

"Uh, Dalton, aren't you a little overdressed for this part of the world?"

He glared at her. "The only time I seem to have the correct clothes on when I'm around you is when we are in bed…"

Thinking about Dalton in bed had her almost as hot as her burned skin. "Why do you have those on now? Going somewhere?"

"I was."

"Well, don't let me hold you up. I can take care of my burn myself."

"I'm not going now. There's no reason to."

"Why?"

They crossed the street and entered his building. "Because I was coming to see you. I was at the airport and I forgot something important. I had to come back and I saw your note."

She reached out to him as the elevator door closed with them in the car.

"Don't touch me, Melanie. If you do, I'll forget that we need to talk. And we *need* to talk."

Melanie let her hand drop. What exhilaration she'd felt at learning he was coming to see her died. This wasn't an open-arms welcome.

The elevator opened and they walked down the hall to his door.

"I know I said some hasty things to you and I'm sorry."

Dalton unlocked the door and pushed it back so she could enter first. "I'm not sorry you did. They were things I needed to hear."

"Still, I didn't have to be so horrible when I said them." She looked around. His place was unbelievable. Ultramodern, with a one-eighty view of the ocean—it was like being outside all the time. One of the windows was a sliding door that was pushed back and a breeze flowed through.

Dalton went into the all-white kitchen and said, "Would you like a glass of iced tea?"

"That would be nice."

He fixed the drinks while she wandered around the living area. It was done in different shades of sand colors with an occasional pop of color.

"Nice place."

"Thank you. I don't spend as much time here as I would like to."

She turned to look at him. "Why is that?"

"It's not much fun to come home to an empty house. I hope to change that, though."

He was making her nervous. Was he trying to tell her that he'd found someone else?

"Look, Dalton, I just came by to say I was sorry about what happened between us. I tried to call you the next day but you were already gone. I just wanted to apologize. I won't keep you any longer." She started for her bag but he stepped between her and it.

"You said Rocket couldn't play."

She looked at him, surprised at the change of subject. "How do you know?"

"I watched the championship game. Even watched the Super Bowl."

"Wow! You have changed."

He moved closer. So close she could feel the heat of his body. "I was so desperate for a glimpse of you I'd sit through anything."

Moisture filled her eyes. She still had a chance.

"I'd like to cash in my rain check. Please kiss me."

Dalton couldn't allow that request to go unfilled, even though they still had things to sort out. He gathered Melanie into his arms and held her tightly as his lips found hers. Damn, he'd missed her with every fiber of his being. She wrapped her arms around his neck and held on as if she would never let go. Her mouth opened for him and she brought her legs up to encircle his hips. Her core called to his hardening manhood.

She pulled her mouth away from his and said, "I've missed you."

"I've missed you too." Dalton carried her to the couch and he sat down. She faced him as she remained in his lap. "We have to talk before this goes any further."

"What's there to talk about?"

"The fact that I love you and want you in my life forever."

She cupped his face and smiled at him. "I love you too."

Dalton's heart soared as he gathered her into his arms again. "Please say it again. I was afraid I'd never hear it."

She looked directly into his eyes. "I love you."

He kissed her. Long, wonderful minutes later, he released her mouth. "When did you decide to come down here?"

"Two days after you left."

He gave her a look of disbelief. "Why did you wait so long?"

"Because I had to wait until after the season was over. Had to work out my contract. Plus I needed to be around to make sure Rocket didn't sneak onto the field or was pushed."

"How did he take not getting to play?"

"Pretty hard at first, but he accepted it was in his best interest. He'll be ready for the next season and not lose his chance to ever play again. I agreed to let him suit up for the Championship game only because I was convinced it would mentally hurt the other team. For the Super Bowl I took no chances. Rocket wore his street clothes on the sideline."

"How about your father? Is he speaking to you?"

"He and Coach Rizzo didn't take it too well. I think winning the Super Bowl, Rocket or not, eased the pain. I quit my job and told my father I was going to work with children. That I wanted to be my own person."

"How did he take that?"

"He's coming around to the idea slowly. But I left on good terms. He gave me a glowing recommendation that helped me get a position at the children's hospital here in Miami. I start next week."

"You do? You were that sure of me?"

"No. Just hopeful."

"Well, I have some confessions of my own."

Her eyes had turned serious. "What are those?"

"You got me thinking about how I've dealt with what happened to me. I went to visit some of the places I lived and thought about how I felt when I lived there. I talked to one of my foster mothers, the one I felt closest to for a time. It was the home where I was the happiest…and the unhappiest. It turns out that the time I lived there in many ways made my life better. She knew what the other kids were doing to me. In her own way she protected me and gave me the groundwork to go on to school and become successful."

"You will have to take me to visit her sometime so I can thank her for the wonderful man I know today."

A knot lodged in his throat at how easy Melanie saw the picture that he'd painted with such broad strokes. "I would love for you to meet Mrs. Richie. I also have a surprise for you."

"What?" Melanie squirmed in his lap and he almost forgot what he was going to say.

"I had a colleague in my practice who specializes in young adults look at Josey Woods's chart. You remember Josey from the day we visited the hospital?"

Melanie nodded.

"Well, there's a new procedure and he thinks she's a perfect candidate. She'll be coming down in the summer to have her legs straightened. She'll be dancing at her prom the next spring."

"Have you talked to her family? Do they have a way to pay? Do I need to do something to help?"

How like Melanie to want to support people.

"That's taken care of. My foundation is covering all their expenses."

She leaned back and studied him. "You have a foundation?"

"I do. Most of the money goes to making foster children's lives better. But since it is mine, I can also use the money for other good causes. All those high fees I charge for my consults go into the foundation."

She kissed him and pulled away. "You really are wonderful."

"Thanks. Coming from you, I consider that the highest of compliments. Now, you mentioned something about a rain check a few minutes ago. If I remember correctly, that was for lovemaking. I'd like to cash that now, if you don't mind."

Melanie rubbed against him. "I don't mind at all. But I just need you to promise that I can come to the bank anytime."

"The doors are always open for you. Now and forever."

EPILOGUE

MELANIE INTERTWINED HER fingers with Dalton's as they sat on her father's couch. He leaned over and kissed her temple.

She looked at the Christmas tree and then around the room at all the people she loved. It was hard to believe that an entire year had passed.

"I hope we don't get snowed in," she said.

Dalton smiled. "If we do, I'm prepared this time. I won't have to borrow your brother's clothes."

"The only reason you are is because I did your packing."

Dalton squeezed her hand. "That's one of the perks of having a wife."

Her father came to sit beside her. "Hey, I saw a piece on the TV about the boy you helped have heart surgery. Smart kid and a big Currents fan."

Melanie squeezed Dalton's hand. His foundation had seen to it that Marcus was able to travel to Miami for the necessary surgery, which was at Melanie's hospital. He had even arranged for his grandmother to come and found them a place to stay for a couple of months afterward. "Marcus is doing great."

She and her father were closer than ever. He had seen to it that she'd had a beautiful wedding with all the trimmings. Her brothers and their families were in attendance.

Even Mrs. Richie was there, proudly sitting in the mother of the groom's spot. Things weren't perfect between Melanie and her father, but they did speak every week on the phone and often talked about things other than football. She and Dalton had also made it up to one of the Currents' games during the year for a visit.

"Present time," one of her nephews called.

As usual it was loud and boisterous as the group unwrapped their presents.

Melanie was handed a box. She looked at the tag and then at Dalton. "We agreed no presents so all the foster kids would have a good Christmas."

"I didn't give you one last year so I owed you. Open it."

Melanie tore the paper away to find a snow globe with Niagara Falls inside.

"I couldn't pass it up."

She smiled at Dalton. "It's perfect. And so are you."

"Uncle Dalton, here's one for you."

He took the small box and looked at the tag. "We said no gifts."

"I couldn't help it either," Melanie said.

Dalton unwrapped the box and opened the top. He lifted the baby's rattle in Currents colors out. "What?"

The room quieted. Melanie watched as question, disbelief, wonder and then pure happiness settled on his face.

"We're having a baby?"

Melanie nodded.

"We're having a baby!" Dalton's arms encircled her as his lips met hers.

Her father said, "Great. Another for the team."

Melanie smiled softly. *No, a family for Dalton.*

* * * * *

MILLS & BOON®
Hardback – November 2015

ROMANCE

A Christmas Vow of Seduction	Maisey Yates
Brazilian's Nine Months' Notice	Susan Stephens
The Sheikh's Christmas Conquest	Sharon Kendrick
Shackled to the Sheikh	Trish Morey
Unwrapping the Castelli Secret	Caitlin Crews
A Marriage Fit for a Sinner	Maya Blake
Larenzo's Christmas Baby	Kate Hewitt
Bought for Her Innocence	Tara Pammi
His Lost-and-Found Bride	Scarlet Wilson
Housekeeper Under the Mistletoe	Cara Colter
Gift-Wrapped in Her Wedding Dress	Kandy Shepherd
The Prince's Christmas Vow	Jennifer Faye
A Touch of Christmas Magic	Scarlet Wilson
Her Christmas Baby Bump	Robin Gianna
Winter Wedding in Vegas	Janice Lynn
One Night Before Christmas	Susan Carlisle
A December to Remember	Sue MacKay
A Father This Christmas?	Louisa Heaton
A Christmas Baby Surprise	Catherine Mann
Courting the Cowboy Boss	Janice Maynard

MILLS & BOON®
Large Print – November 2015

ROMANCE

The Ruthless Greek's Return	Sharon Kendrick
Bound by the Billionaire's Baby	Cathy Williams
Married for Amari's Heir	Maisey Yates
A Taste of Sin	Maggie Cox
Sicilian's Shock Proposal	Carol Marinelli
Vows Made in Secret	Louise Fuller
The Sheikh's Wedding Contract	Andie Brock
A Bride for the Italian Boss	Susan Meier
The Millionaire's True Worth	Rebecca Winters
The Earl's Convenient Wife	Marion Lennox
Vettori's Damsel in Distress	Liz Fielding

HISTORICAL

A Rose for Major Flint	Louise Allen
The Duke's Daring Debutante	Ann Lethbridge
Lord Laughraine's Summer Promise	Elizabeth Beacon
Warrior of Ice	Michelle Willingham
A Wager for the Widow	Elisabeth Hobbes

MEDICAL

Always the Midwife	Alison Roberts
Midwife's Baby Bump	Susanne Hampton
A Kiss to Melt Her Heart	Emily Forbes
Tempted by Her Italian Surgeon	Louisa George
Daring to Date Her Ex	Annie Claydon
The One Man to Heal Her	Meredith Webber

MILLS & BOON®
Hardback – December 2015

ROMANCE

The Price of His Redemption	Carol Marinelli
Back in the Brazilian's Bed	Susan Stephens
The Innocent's Sinful Craving	Sara Craven
Brunetti's Secret Son	Maya Blake
Talos Claims His Virgin	Michelle Smart
Destined for the Desert King	Kate Walker
Ravensdale's Defiant Captive	Melanie Milburne
Caught in His Gilded World	Lucy Ellis
The Best Man & The Wedding Planner	Teresa Carpenter
Proposal at the Winter Ball	Jessica Gilmore
Bodyguard...to Bridegroom?	Nikki Logan
Christmas Kisses with Her Boss	Nina Milne
Playboy Doc's Mistletoe Kiss	Tina Beckett
Her Doctor's Christmas Proposal	Louisa George
From Christmas to Forever?	Marion Lennox
A Mummy to Make Christmas	Susanne Hampton
Miracle Under the Mistletoe	Jennifer Taylor
His Christmas Bride-to-Be	Abigail Gordon
Lone Star Holiday Proposal	Yvonne Lindsay
A Baby for the Boss	Maureen Child

MILLS & BOON®
Large Print – December 2015

ROMANCE

The Greek Demands His Heir	Lynne Graham
The Sinner's Marriage Redemption	Annie West
His Sicilian Cinderella	Carol Marinelli
Captivated by the Greek	Julia James
The Perfect Cazorla Wife	Michelle Smart
Claimed for His Duty	Tara Pammi
The Marakaios Baby	Kate Hewitt
Return of the Italian Tycoon	Jennifer Faye
His Unforgettable Fiancée	Teresa Carpenter
Hired by the Brooding Billionaire	Kandy Shepherd
A Will, a Wish...a Proposal	Jessica Gilmore

HISTORICAL

Griffin Stone: Duke of Decadence	Carole Mortimer
Rake Most Likely to Thrill	Bronwyn Scott
Under a Desert Moon	Laura Martin
The Bootlegger's Daughter	Lauri Robinson
The Captain's Frozen Dream	Georgie Lee

MEDICAL

Midwife...to Mum!	Sue MacKay
His Best Friend's Baby	Susan Carlisle
Italian Surgeon to the Stars	Melanie Milburne
Her Greek Doctor's Proposal	Robin Gianna
New York Doc to Blushing Bride	Janice Lynn
Still Married to Her Ex!	Lucy Clark

MILLS & BOON®

Why shop at millsandboon.co.uk?

Each year, thousands of romance readers find their perfect read at millsandboon.co.uk. That's because we're passionate about bringing you the very best romantic fiction. Here are some of the advantages of shopping at www.millsandboon.co.uk:

* **Get new books first**—you'll be able to buy your favourite books one month before they hit the shops

* **Get exclusive discounts**—you'll also be able to buy our specially created monthly collections, with up to 50% off the RRP

* **Find your favourite authors**—latest news, interviews and new releases for all your favourite authors and series on our website, plus ideas for what to try next

* **Join in**—once you've bought your favourite books, don't forget to register with us to rate, review and join in the discussions

Visit **www.millsandboon.co.uk**
for all this and more today!